"It's not that I don't want to kiss you..." Daniel began.

"You *want* to kiss me?" Jenny asked, joy flooding her soul.

"Yes, from the first moment I saw you, but—"

Sadness had replaced joy in her face. "Sometimes I wish I could have just one kiss...a small one...so I'll know what it's like."

Daniel's hands trembled as he cupped her face. "Just a small kiss between friends, then," he murmured, drawn into the luminous blue of her eyes. *Would he have the strength to stop at one kiss?*

When her lips moved under his, he knew that it was right, and he wanted more, cradling her against his chest.

"I didn't know kissing would feel like falling," Jenny said softly. "Then I felt like I was flying." She traced his mouth with her fingertips. "Daniel, you've made my dreams come true...."

WHAT ARE *LOVESWEPT* ROMANCES?

They are stories of true romance and touching emotion. We believe those two very important ingredients are constants in our highly sensual and very believable stories in the LOVESWEPT line. Our goal is to give you, the reader, stories of consistently high quality that may sometimes make you laugh, sometimes make you cry, but are always fresh and creative and contain many delightful surprises within their pages.

Most romance fans read an enormous number of books. Those they truly love, they keep. Others may be traded with friends and soon forgotten. We hope that each LOVESWEPT romance will be a treasure—a "keeper." We will always try to publish

LOVE STORIES YOU'LL NEVER FORGET BY AUTHORS YOU'LL ALWAYS REMEMBER

The Editors

656

A PRINCE FOR JENNY

PEGGY WEBB

BANTAM BOOKS
NEW YORK · TORONTO · LONDON · SYDNEY · AUCKLAND

A PRINCE FOR JENNY

A Bantam Book / December 1993

*LOVESWEPT and the wave design are registered
trademarks of Bantam Books, a division of
Bantam Doubleday Dell Publishing Group, Inc.
Registered in U.S. Patent
and Trademark Office and elsewhere.*

*All rights reserved.
Copyright © 1993 by Peggy Webb.
Cover art copyright © 1993 by Ed Tadiello.
No part of this book may be reproduced or transmitted
in any form or by any means, electronic or mechanical,
including photocopying, recording, or by any
information storage and retrieval system, without
permission in writing from the publisher.
For information address: Bantam Books.*

If you purchased this book without a cover you should be aware that this book is stolen property. It was reported as "unsold and destroyed" to the publisher and neither the author nor the publisher has received any payment for this "stripped book."

If you would be interested in receiving protective vinyl covers for your Loveswept books, please write to this address for information:

*Loveswept
Bantam Books
P.O. Box 985
Hicksville, NY 11802*

ISBN 0-553-44341-0

Published simultaneously in the United States and Canada

Bantam Books are published by Bantam Books, a division of Bantam Doubleday Dell Publishing Group, Inc. Its trademark, consisting of the words "Bantam Books" and the portrayal of a rooster, is Registered in U.S. Patent and Trademark Office and in other countries. Marca Registrada. Bantam Books, 1540 Broadway, New York, New York 10036.

PRINTED IN THE UNITED STATES OF AMERICA

OPM   0 9 8 7 6 5 4 3 2 1

Once again in memory of Cooper,
who was special in so many ways,
and in honor of her grandparents
Jack and Shirley, who understand
the true meaning of love.

ONE

"Mr. Sullivan, that tight-lipped fool your children call a nanny has fainted dead away on the floor . . ."

Holding the telephone in a death grip, Daniel Sullivan bolted from his chair and stood glowering at the yellow roses on his desk. The woman on the other end of the line went on without pausing for breath.

" . . . and looks as though she won't be able to navigate her way to the bathroom, let alone get your children home, and I'm calling to see what you want me to do about them."

"Who the hell are you?"

"Watch your language, Mr. Sullivan. You're talking to an old woman." She didn't sound old: She sounded spry and decidedly wicked as she chuckled into the phone. "I'm Gwendolyn

2

Phepps, Miss Jenny Love-Townsend's executive assistant."

Daniel cursed under his breath. If his secretary weren't out there pouring champagne to a bunch of hand-kissing bigwigs, he'd have known who she was. Hell, he wouldn't even be talking to her. Helen would have taken care of everything.

"Where are my children now, Miss Phepps?"

"They're with Jenny in the backyard."

What kind of secretary was she? Calling her boss Jenny? The dossier had listed Jenny Love-Townsend as the best portrait artist in the nation. You'd think she'd run a tighter ship.

"I'll be there in fifteen minutes. Stay right where you are."

Daniel slammed down the phone and grabbed his jacket. Then he pushed open the door of his office and waded through the mob attending the open house to find his secretary. The mayor and the chief of police had her cornered over by the fireplace.

Daniel lifted one eyebrow, and she came running.

"Mr. Sullivan?" She pressed her hand over her heart. "I wondered where you'd disappeared to."

"I didn't disappear; I was hiding."

"Mr. *Sullivan* . . . from your own guests?"

"I just pay for the games, Miss Gibbs. I don't

have to mix and mingle with the players." He explained where he was going. "Make my apologies."

"I always do."

He took the Corvette and roared out of the company garage, hell-bent for leather. The modest shops and quaint restaurants of Florence, Alabama, blurred together as he whizzed by. He didn't take the time to look, didn't even *care* to look. Florence was just another city to conquer, another base for Sullivan Enterprises; Alabama just another state to put between himself and Claire Louise Montague Sullivan.

The portrait studio was located in a quiet neighborhood on the outskirts of the city. A hand-painted wooden sign proclaiming simply The Studio stood in front of an old-fashioned house with a wraparound veranda, fanlight door, and ornately carved cornices.

A woman who had to be Gwendolyn Phepps met him at the door. She looked as feisty as she'd sounded. Tight corkscrew curls dyed a bright yellow bounced around a face lined with age. Her massive hips were encased in dungarees, and her sweatshirt sported a hand-painted frog and the slogan, You have to kiss a few frogs before you meet your prince.

4

"Well, Daniel Sullivan, if you're not a sight for sore eyes." She tipped her head back and squinted up at him. "I can see why the whole town's buzzing. Especially the females."

"Miss Phepps, I presume."

She threw back her head and roared with laughter. "Damned if you don't sound like something out of a bad English movie."

A pompous ass. That's what he sounded like, but it served its purpose.

She stepped aside to let him in. The entry hall was wide and gracious, with polished wooden floors, beaded wood walls painted white, and Miss Nell Williams propped up in the corner looking green.

He knelt beside his children's nanny and took her limp wrist. "Miss Williams, are you all right?"

"I'm sorry, Mr. Sullivan." She pressed a washcloth to her forehead.

"No need to be sorry. I'll call a doctor."

"No," she said, attempting to rise. Daniel helped her up and led her to a chair. "I'm not sick, just a little woozy, that's all."

"She didn't mind the dogs," Gwendolyn said, bustling in with a glass of water. "She didn't even mind the cats. It was the guinea pigs that did her in."

"Guinea pigs?"

"Franklin and Eleanor." She thrust the water at Miss Williams. "Roosevelt," she added grinning. "Jenny loves animals."

Maybe he should have read that dossier more closely. He'd meant to send his children to a portrait studio, not to a zoo.

"Where are my children?"

"Out back." Gwendolyn Phepps nodded toward a door at the end of the hallway. "I'll take care of the swooning nanny, but I'm warning you, don't bother Jenny if she's painting. It breaks her concentration."

Painting portraits in the backyard? He'd bother her all right. He was going to get his children and go to somebody who knew how to pose them on a large velvet settee and create a portrait worthy of hanging over a marble fireplace.

He strode down the hall and pushed open the back door, expecting the worst. What he saw took his breath away.

His two children were flying through the air in rope swings, their voices bright with laughter. And beside them was the most exquisite creature he'd ever seen. Her white skirt billowed around shapely legs that were all woman, but her hair framed a face that was more heavenly than earthly, more angel than mortal. The wind caught her laughter as she swayed back and forth in the swing, and Daniel thought of bells, silver bells like those he'd heard somewhere in a church in the Alps.

"Go high, Jenny, go high," his daughter Megan chanted.

"Yeah, *real* high," Patrick chimed in.

"Let's go high together." There was an odd, breathless catch in Jenny's voice, but it had the lilt of music. She touched one delicate foot to the ground and pushed off, sending her swing gliding through the summer air.

Standing in the doorway, drinking in the sight of her like a poor desert wanderer who'd discovered water, Daniel heard snatches of some long-forgotten lullaby. At first he thought he must be dreaming, then he realized the music was real.

Jenny was humming.

It was an Irish lullaby his grandmother had sung to him when he was a child no older than Patrick and Megan, a song so fraught with memories that tears burned the back of Daniel's eyes. If he'd had a heart, he'd say that Jenny touched it; but everybody knew Daniel Sullivan didn't have a heart.

Impatient with himself for being a sentimental fool, he swung wide the door and stepped into Jenny's backyard. It was an enchanted place worthy of the woman in the swing, a fairyland of graceful willow trees and fragrant flowers and white wicker furniture with cushions the color of the sky. Jenny's easel was set up beside a white wicker stool, and swaths of pastel-colored oils streaked the white canvas. Even a utilitarian type like Daniel could see that the finished painting would be as exquisite as its artist.

The three in the swings were having so much fun, they didn't even see him.

"Megan . . . Patrick . . . watch this." Jenny set her swing in a circular motion. The ropes twisted tightly together, then released in a quick burst that sent Jenny spinning round and round.

Fascinated, Daniel stood beside a wicker chair watching. What manner of woman was she?

Her hair whipped loose from its pins and spread across her face in a pale golden curtain. A capricious breeze lifted her bow and sailed it through the air. It landed with a plop in Daniel's outstretched hand.

Holding the bit of satin as if it were a burnt offering, Daniel started toward the swings.

"Daddy . . . Daddy," his children called, racing toward him. They tagged him on the legs, then raced on, chasing each other around the yard.

Jenny dug her feet into the ground, and her swing came to a bone-jarring halt. For a moment she sat very still, then slowly she lifted one delicate hand and parted the hair covering her face.

"Oh," she said, peeking through her curtain of hair, her mouth deliciously rounded and her face as rosy as the flowers climbing the trellis behind her swing.

"I didn't know women still blushed."

"I'm . . ." Her face got even pinker when she saw her hair ribbon in his hand. She patted her hair as if searching for the bow might miraculously send it back to its rightful place. "I seem to have lost my bow."

She tilted her head to one side and looked at Daniel with eyes so wide and blue and innocent, he was almost taken in.

"And I seem to have found it." He held it out, and for a moment he thought she wasn't even going to take it. Then she reached out shyly, almost like a child. Her fingers brushed his skin with a touch as delicate as the wings of a butterfly.

"Thank you," she said. Prim. Proper. Like a lady. Daniel wasn't fooled. Nobody was that innocent.

Jenny caught her hair and anchored it back with the ribbon. She put the bow in crooked, and then smiled up at him.

"Thank you," she said again with that breathy, lilting voice. The rakish angle of the bow made her look like a mischievous imp. An *innocent*, mischievous imp. He wondered what her game was. "I'm Jenny."

"Daniel Sullivan. Miss Phepps said I'd find you here."

"Gwendolyn... Yes, I like to paint in the garden. Especially children. They're like the flowers..."

She stood up, tall and elegant and so close, her soft skirt brushed against his leg. For a moment he was caught up in the nearness of her, her delicate face and heart-shaped mouth and sweet scent.

"... like this lovely yellow rose." She reached up and touched the boutonniere his secretary had made him wear to that damned open house.

Her hand lingered on the rose, and she was so close, he could see each separate eyelash and the fine, silken texture of her skin, and the tiny drop of moisture on her lip where she touched it with the end of her tongue.

He *did* have a heart, after all. It was probably cast iron, but it was beating such a rhythm, he figured Jenny Love-Townsend could hear. She was tempting, dangerous. He stepped back, determined not to be seduced by her feminine wiles.

She blushed again, then without a word turned away and started toward her easel. There was an odd little hitch to her walk, as if she had a leg injury. But he'd seen her legs, had stared at them like some besotted fool while her skirt blew round them in the wind. They were perfect. Beautiful.

"I suppose you want to see the portrait."

"Yes." He approached her cautiously, stopping close enough to see but not close enough to touch. Jenny lifted the canvas and held it toward him, smiling expectantly. "I'm a businessman, Miss Townsend..."

"Just Jenny... please."

"You could be drawing a pig in a poke there, for all I know." At her crestfallen look, he hurried to make amends. "But I'm sure it will be a wonderful portrait. I'm told you're the best."

"My talent is not mine. It's a gift. I treat it the way all gifts should be treated... with great care."

There was no rebuke in her voice, not even of the most gentle kind, but he suddenly felt guilty and ashamed, as if he'd taken some precious gift and treated it with careless disregard.

She held the portrait between them a moment longer, watching him with such intensity that he began to think she was seeing all the way through to his shriveled soul. Finally she turned and put the canvas back on the easel, and Daniel breathed a sigh of relief.

"I understand you'll need the children back for further sittings?"

"Yes. Some artists work from photographs. I have to see life to paint life."

He wondered how much life she had seen, this beguiling, ephemeral-looking woman in her Victorian dress and her lopsided hair ribbon. Then he was angry at himself for wondering.

Turning quickly, he summoned his children. "Megan! Patrick!" They raced to his side, their cheeks whipped pink by the wind and the sun, and their eyes bright with laughter. He hoped Jenny captured their sense of wonder and innocence, for he knew how soon it would fade. "Go inside and wait with Miss Williams."

They started off at a trot.

"And don't run in the house."

"We won't, Daddy." Megan, the ringleader, spoke for both of them. He could tell by the tone of her voice that she'd race through Jenny's polished hallways as soon as she got out of sight.

The child-rearing books didn't tell what to do about things like that.

" 'Bye." Jenny waved at them.

" 'Bye, Jenny. Pet Eleanor for me." Megan, the animal lover.

He watched his children through the door, then turned back to Jenny. The impact of her hit him afresh, and she blushed under his gaze. He rammed the hand that had held her hair ribbon into his pocket.

"Will this time next week do?"

"Tomorrow. Once I start a project, I like to work straight through."

"Miss Williams took a turn for the worse when she saw your menagerie, so I'll have to get someone else to bring them back."

"I hope it's you."

In spite of her stunning candor, she looked completely artless, and for a heady moment he felt like some damned hero. He decided there were things in her dossier that had been left out. Not only was she the best portrait artist in America, she was the best actress.

"I'm a busy man, Miss Townsend. I don't have time to waste sitting on wicker chairs in flower gardens."

"I'm so sorry," she said, looking for all the world as if she meant it.

Daniel was close to cursing, but some foolish sense of nobility kept him from doing it in front of her.

"You'll have the children this time tomorrow." He didn't even say good-bye, but hurried toward the house as if demons were on his tail. He supposed they were, the twin demons of passion and fear.

A Prince for Jenny

13

"Come again," she called after him in that sweet, halting voice.

Who was she, this woman who had so easily pierced his armor and gone straight to his heart? He intended to find out, but he had no intention of coming again. Once was enough to suffer over a woman who claimed innocence, then cut out your heart with a dull butcher knife.

He collected the children and their nanny, then dropped Miss Williams off at her house and drove to his office. He'd send someone for her car.

"Daddy, can I have a guinea pig?" Megan bounced up and down on the sofa in his office, her dark curls bobbing.

"We'll see."

"That means no," Patrick piped up. He was sprawled on the carpet with his coloring book, his handsome little face screwed up in concentration.

"It does not," Megan shot back.

"Does too."

"Children, don't argue. We'll talk about a guinea pig when we get home." There should be a mother at home waiting to help with that conversation. "Daddy has some work to do right now."

"Promise?" Megan tilted her head to one side and looked up at him with a pretty pout on her lips. Daniel's gut clenched. She was so like her mother that it was all he could do to keep from getting into his plane, flying out to Atlanta, and dragging Claire back by the hair of her head.

"I promise, sweetheart."

Satisfied, she plopped beside her brother and took up her crayons.

He stood watching them for a while, filled with such pride and love, he couldn't bear to turn away. At least Claire hadn't asked for custody of the children. He'd have seen her in hell before giving them up.

Turning away, he got a thick sheaf of papers from his desk drawer and began to read. Jenny Love-Townsend. Thirty-four years old. Natural daughter of Sarah Love Townsend and adopted daughter of Jake Townsend, the publishing magnate. Portrait artist of presidents and kings.

Nothing new there. He'd read it before he'd sent his children to her. Like all powerful, wealthy men, he trusted his children to no one who failed to pass his strict and careful scrutiny.

A vision of Jenny touching the yellow rose on his lapel came to him. He put his hand on the wilted rose and stood looking out the window. The sun was setting over the city, shading it with purple and turning the river to gold. He felt once again the whisper of Jenny's skirt against his legs.

With a muttered curse, he jerked the rose off and tossed it into the garbage can, then he turned his attention back to the dossier. There must be something he'd missed.

He skimmed the information about schooling and religious and political preferences. Suddenly he stilled. There it was. *There*. A tiny asterisk, referring to a footnote on the back page.

Daniel turned to the final page and honed in on the footnote. It was one line. *Jenny Love-Townsend was born special.*

He put the dossier into his desk drawer, then sank into his chair and bowed his head.

"Daddy?" Megan's little arms went around his neck. "Are you all right?"

"Yes, sweetheart. I'm all right."

He had to lie, for how could he explain heartsickness to a little child?

TWO

Jenny stood in her flower garden long after Daniel Sullivan had departed. If she took one small step, she'd be standing exactly where he'd stood.

She pressed her hand over her trembling lips, then glanced toward the window to see if Gwendolyn was looking. There was no sign of her.

Jenny took the step and then stood with her toes curled under. Excitement coursed through her, and the heady sense of having found something she'd been looking for all her life.

Daniel Sullivan had worn a yellow rose. Somehow she'd known he would.

Her one and only hero, the man she loved best in all the world, had appeared in her backyard long ago bearing a yellow rose. She'd been four at the time, and she'd loved Jake

Townsend from the minute he'd handed her the rose.

Jenny closed her eyes, letting the feel of being near Daniel seep through the soles of her feet and all the way up to her heart. She could see his face as clearly as if he were standing beside her.

Daniel Sullivan. Her hero.

She stood where he had a while longer, holding on to the delicious sense of wonder, then she got her sketch pad from beside the easel and sat on the wicker love seat. Bent over so that her hair brushed against the paper, she captured Daniel Sullivan with quick, deft strokes—his square jaw, his noble nose, his bold eyebrows and fierce dark eyes, his shock of wild black hair that looked as if he'd just climbed down from a mountain and couldn't be bothered with a comb, his mouth . . .

Her pencil stilled, and Jenny gazed across the yard at the pink roses climbing the trellis behind the swings. His mouth was beautifully defined, mobile and generous, with a full lower lip. Just thinking about it made Jenny's breath catch.

His mouth was so beautiful, she wasn't sure she could ever get it right on paper. Her hand trembled as she touched pencil to paper once more.

"Jenny?"

Startled, she looked up. Gwendolyn had come

into the yard, carrying a tray of lemonade and cookies.

"I thought you might like a snack." Her oldest and dearest friend sat on the love seat and leaned over to look at the sketch. There was no mistaking the likeness, and Gwendolyn was nobody's fool. She pursed her lips over the drawing, then glanced up to study Jenny's face.

A robin hopped across the grass looking for worms, and a pair of cardinals landed on the willow tree and set the branch to swaying. Jenny reached for a cookie.

"Is that a preliminary sketch for a portrait?"

"No. I just wanted to draw him."

"You've captured him to a tee." Gwendolyn munched on her own cookie. "He's not pretty, but there's something powerful and magnetic about him. Dangerous, I'd say." She shot a sly look at Jenny.

"He's a nice man."

"You don't know that, Jenny."

"I do. I know it in here." Jenny put both hands over her heart.

Gently Gwendolyn took one of Jenny's hands in hers and caressed the long, slender fingers. "You're sheltered, honey. You've always been surrounded by people who are kind and loving . . . your mother, your sister and two brothers, me, Jake. . . . God knows, Jake Townsend would kill anybody who wasn't kind to you."

"Daniel will always be kind."

The stillness in the garden was absolute, broken only by the call of the cardinal and a deep sigh from Gwendolyn.

"Jenny . . . Jenny." Gwendolyn squeezed her hand. "I don't want you to be hurt."

With her fingertips, Jenny traced the penciled lines of Daniel's face. Megan had said her mother ran away. How could any woman run away from a man like that?

Her hand lingered over the sensual lines of Daniel's mouth. She'd never been kissed, but from the time she'd peeked around the nursery door and seen Jake kissing her mother, she'd known it must be something wonderful.

Oh, she knew she was different. Inside her mind, everything worked fine. She just had a hard time getting it all out. Normal men like Daniel didn't kiss women like her, and they certainly didn't fall in love. But that was all right.

All she wanted to do was love. She didn't expect to be loved back.

"Dreaming won't hurt, Gwendolyn."

"As long as you know it's only a dream."

Daniel sat at the head of the carved dining table that had belonged to three generations of

Sullivans before him. His children sat on either side of him, dressed for dinner as he always insisted. Candles gleamed on the long expanse of polished walnut, sparkling rainbows on the crystal that had belonged to his grandmother.

Three was a lonely number at a table designed for fourteen. Daniel tried not to think about it.

"Can we talk about the guinea pigs now, Daddy?" Megan asked. "You said right after dessert."

"So I did." He leaned back in his chair and studied his children over his steepled fingers. "Why do you want a guinea pig?"

" 'Cause Jenny has one," Megan said.

"That's not a good enough reason."

Patrick regarded him with solemn eyes. " 'Cause Mommy runned away."

Guilt smote Daniel . . . and pain. He'd failed to give his children the one thing they needed most—a stable home with two loving parents. *You're selfish*, Claire had screamed at him when he'd gone after her to bring her back. *I don't intend to spend the rest of my life waiting for you to come home from your almighty job.* He'd flagellated himself for months for neglecting a woman so beautiful, so attentive, so innocent . . . until he'd discovered her in the arms of another man.

Even so, he still sometimes wondered if he

could have done something different, something to make her want to stay.

He cleared away the lump in his throat, but he couldn't clear that last twisted image of Claire wrapped in the arms of her lover.

His son's words hung in the air, and the three of them were trapped in the ugly web he and Claire had woven. It was Megan, the peacemaker, who broke the spell.

"That's okay, Daddy, 'cause we got you." Megan grinned, then skipped around the table and hugged his neck. "I want two guinea pigs, 'cause Jenny says animals need friends just like people, and I'll call mine Mable and Patrick can name his Charles, and we'll take *really, really* good care of them and hug them every day and give them lots and lots of food and they won't ever leave, and now can I please be excused? I have to go to the bathroom."

"You may." He'd been wrapped around his daughter's finger . . . as he always was. He smiled at his son.

"Someday your sister is going to strike fear in the hearts of that stodgy old board at Sullivan Enterprises."

"Are you soggy, Daddy?"

"The word is 'stodgy,' Patrick. It means . . ."

"Will you sing the Irish songs to me?" Patrick came around the table and climbed into his lap, then cuddled his downy cheek against Daniel's.

Megan popped her head around the door. "Not till I get back." She danced up and down on one leg. "I'll hurry."

Daniel wondered if he'd ever be adequate to the task of bringing up his children alone.

When his daughter got back, he sang "Too-ra-loo-ra-loo-ral" and their favorite, "Danny Boy," the song his grandmother used to sing to him. After she'd sung, she would hug him close and say, "I love you, my Danny boy." Her love was the only constant he'd had. So far away and so long ago.

When the last notes of "Danny Boy" died, he kissed his children and whispered, "I love you, Megan and Patrick."

Did they understand that his love was real and that he'd never go away and leave them? He hoped so.

Afterward the children played quietly until bedtime, then Daniel carried them both up the stairs and tucked them in. He could easily have afforded for the nanny to live in, but he wanted their lives to be as normal as possible. He couldn't take the place of a mother who had abandoned them, but he could try.

He took one last look at the precious faces of

his children, then went to his downstairs study and poured himself a brandy.

With his glass in his hand, he stood at the window and watched the shadows of the moon in the front yard. The stone face of the angel in the water fountain gleamed soft and silvery, her smile haunting and almost real. Suddenly Daniel remembered another face, another smile.

Jenny. With eyes impossibly blue and innocent voice lifted in Irish melody. Beautiful Jenny, fatally flawed in the eyes of the world, calling to him in a voice so sweet, it brought tears to his eyes.

Come again . . . come again.

He'd be a fool to listen, for he understood all too well the consequences of folly.

"The blue or the green?"

Gwendolyn looked up from the coffee she was making. Jenny stood in the doorway holding two dresses, one the color of spring leaves and the other the exact shade of her eyes. The morning sun slanted across her hair, turning it to spun gold. Soft color bloomed on her cheeks and in her lips.

"Don't you think those dresses are a little too fancy to paint in?"

"I want to look nice for Daniel."

Gwendolyn's heart was so full that she couldn't speak. She busied herself pouring coffee into two mugs. Out of the corner of her eye, she could still see Jenny standing in the doorway with that look of bright expectancy on her face.

"He's a busy man, you know, head of that big company, and all. He might not come."

Jenny laid the green dress across the back of a chair and, holding the blue one close, whirled around and around the room, bumping into chairs. When she was near the window, she steadied herself on the windowsill, laughing.

"I think I'll wear the blue. Daniel likes blue."

"How do you know?"

"I know in here." She covered her heart with her hand.

Oh, Jenny. Jenny. Gwendolyn sank into her chair and took a sip of coffee. She was too old for this job.

Jenny took a sip of her coffee, then drifted back up the stairs, holding on to the party dresses. Gwendolyn pressed her hand over her massive bosom.

Dreaming won't hurt, Jenny had said.

Gwendolyn prayed to God she was right, for if dreaming *did* hurt, they'd all have Jake Townsend to answer to.

25

When the clock said three, Jenny poured tea into two porcelain cups, then carried them into the garden and sat at the table, waiting for Daniel.

Gwendolyn stood at the window not knowing what to do. A part of her wanted to go out and gather Jenny and her teacups, then bring her inside and tell her as gently as she could that Daniel Sullivan would never show up in the flower garden for afternoon tea, that men like him paid court to women who fit in their fast-paced, sophisticated worlds. Another part of her wanted to march into Sullivan Enterprises and drag Daniel Sullivan out by the ear and force him to take tea in the garden with Jenny—and to smile while he did it.

The hands of the clock inched around to quarter after. Outside in the garden, Jenny was oblivious to time. She guarded the teacups from a dragonfly determined to use them as a landing pad, and laughed at the antics of that crotchety old mockingbird scolding a pair of robins.

Inside the kitchen, Gwendolyn squeezed her hands together and watched. This business was bound to drive her to an early grave.

Daniel sat in his parked car with his hands sweating, like some teenager full of fear and hormones. Glancing into the rearview mirror, he ran a hand through his hair. Maybe he should have taken the time to shower and change.

Hell, he was acting as if this were a damned date and not a last-minute attack of conscience that had sent him scurrying to Jenny's yard instead of sending Helen as he'd intended. If he'd followed his head instead of his heart, he'd be sitting in his office right now. Safe.

"Daddy, aren't we *ever* going inside?" Megan, the impatient one. "I want to pet the guinea pigs before Jenny paints."

"All right, children. Let's go." He glanced at his watch. Three-thirty. He'd be out of there in five minutes.

Gwendolyn met him at the door. The children raced off to see the guinea pigs, and he faced Jenny's executive assistant.

"She's waiting for you in the garden," she said. "Wipe that scowl off your face."

"It matches the one on yours."

"Let's get this straight: Jenny sees you through the eyes of innocence, but I don't. I don't know why you came back. All I know is that if you do or say anything to hurt her, I'll personally run you out of town on a rail."

"Miss Phepps, I can assure you my motives are pure."

"Good. Keep them that way."

The minute he saw Jenny, he knew he'd lied. She was sitting at the white wicker table wearing a feminine dress that matched her eyes and a bright smile that rivaled the sun. He hadn't come merely to see that his children arrived safely; he'd come to see Jenny's smile.

"Hello." She rose, graceful as a willow. "I knew you'd come."

"Hello, Jenny."

"Say it again." Pressing her hands over her heart, she spoke in a breathy, wistful voice.

"Hello . . ."

"No. My name."

"Jenny . . ."

"Again," she whispered.

"Jenny . . ."

Her name was music on his lips, part litany of praise, part litany of supplication, and he had the sensation of falling, falling straight into her blue eyes, through their golden center all the way to the magic that lay beyond. Wind stirred her hair and the filmy skirt that rustled around her legs. One delicate finger touched her lips.

He stood breathless at the wonder of it all.

"I made tea," she said.

Two china cups sat upon the table. And two lace-edged napkins. Sitting down, she lifted one of the cups and offered it up to him. How could he refuse?

"That's kind of you, Jenny." He sat at the wicker table, feeling too big and unaccountably ill at ease. When he took the teacup, her soft hand touched his, and he felt an astonishing shock of awareness.

To cover, he took a sip of tea. It was cold.

"This is delicious."

She smiled as if he'd awarded her a great prize. "Mother taught me how to make tea. It was a long time ago. I couldn't read very well, but I could make tea."

He pictured her as a little girl, struggling with the printed word, probably frustrated. How wise her mother had been to teach her something at which she could excel.

"Your mother must be a lovely woman."

"She is . . . and lucky too. She has Jake. Sometimes they dance in the moonlight."

The wistful quality of her voice tore at his heart. He studied her, the golden hair that would gleam in the moonlight, the silky skin that would be soft to the touch, the heart-shaped lips that would taste so sweet. Feelings stirred deep within him, feelings that had nothing to do with compassion but everything to do with a man wanting a woman.

"Do you dance in the moonlight, Daniel?"

"I used to." A century ago, it seemed.

"How wonderful that must be." Jenny glanced

down at her lap. "My brothers tried to teach me once, but I'm too clumsy to dance."

"You're as graceful as the dandelions that dance on the summer breeze... and twice as pretty in that lovely blue dress."

"Thank you." Softly, she reached out and touched his hand. "You're a nice man."

As she rubbed a delicate finger across his knuckles, Daniel imagined himself whirling her around in the moonlight, holding her lithe body close so she wouldn't stumble. Passion stirred his loins, and he mentally pulled himself back from the brink. God in heaven, what was he thinking of? Casting himself in the role of hero, of somebody who would ride up on a white charger and rescue her from her burden of innocence.

Her hand burned on his, but he gladly suffered the pain. Never again would he use his stinger on her, for Jenny was more than born special: She was special in ways he dared not even think about.

"I'm glad you came, Daniel."

"I'm glad too." Was he? A part of him was turning cartwheels at the sheer ecstasy of being in her sweet presence, but a part of him was weeping.

"You will stay while I paint the children?"

"Yes." Sullivan Enterprises seemed another world away, and suddenly not so very important.

"I knew you would." She stood, smiling down at him, with her hand resting gently on his shoulder. "And afterward, we'll all have a tea party."

Daniel was overwhelmed, a prisoner of her tender touch and innocent expectations. He sat in her delicate wicker chair sipping the cold tea while she tamed his two hellions with gentle persuasion.

"Let's swing." She climbed aboard a rope swing as happy as a child herself. His children's joyous laughter drifted upward, then Jenny left her swing and took up her brush.

Her hands flew over the canvas, as fragile looking as two snowbirds, but swift and sure. When she finally laid the brushes aside, he was amazed that he'd watched for an hour instead of only minutes.

"Are you ready for a tea party?" Jenny asked his children.

"Yeah!" They raced to her and caught her hands, with Megan grinning up at her and asking, "Can the animals come too?"

"Yes. Go inside and bring them out, and I'll get the cookies and tea."

She started across the yard, an enchanting woman who made Daniel forget everything except the magic of being in her presence.

"I'll help," he said, under her spell. And that's

A Prince for Jenny

how he found himself in the kitchen pouring tea into tiny cups and laughing.

Later they ended up sitting in a lopsided circle on the grass—Megan holding onto Eleanor and Franklin, the guinea pigs, Patrick hugging Ruby and Marilyn, the prissy Persians, and Jenny cuddling Ralph and Ernest, the fluffy mutts.

Daniel sat beside Jenny, feeling a contentment he hadn't known in years.

"It's peaceful in your garden, Jenny."

"I love gardens. The birds and the flowers don't mind that I'm different." There was quiet dignity in her voice and not a shred of self-pity.

The world was full of thoughtless cruelty, especially for people who didn't fit the norm, and the idea that Jenny had suffered filled Daniel with helpless rage. He tried to think of a response that wouldn't sound condescending.

"I don't care if Jenny's taller," Megan said. "Do you, Daddy?"

"Not in the least." He'd never been prouder of his daughter. "We don't mind if she's prettier than other people either, do we?"

"Nope."

"And more talented?" Out of the corner of his eye, he could see joy bloom across Jenny's face. Daniel felt as if he'd won an Olympic gold medal.

"Nope."

"See, Jenny. We're like the birds and the flowers." He turned to her, smiling, and suddenly he got lost in her blue eyes. "We like you exactly the way you are."

"And I like you." She touched his hand softly. "I think you're wonderful."

He wasn't, not by a long shot. His father knew it; Claire knew. But being called wonderful felt damned good, and so he kept sitting in the flower garden when plain common sense told him he ought to go. Was he selfish to want Jenny to keep thinking of him as wonderful?

"Daniel." Jenny leaned close to him, her face rosy. "Do you dream?"

Cynical men didn't dream, but he didn't tell Jenny that. Instead he said, "Do you?"

"Yes, I dream about going off to see the world." She got a faraway look in her eyes. "I'll drive myself, so I can stop in the woods and wade in the rivers and sit under the trees and listen to the birds. And I'll go in a bus big enough for my animals."

He doubted that she could drive a car, let alone a bus, but he pretended to believe in her vision.

"That sounds like a wonderful idea, Jenny," he said, and meant it. "Usually when I travel, I race along the interstates from motel to motel, seeing nothing but fast-food restaurants and shopping malls."

"Can you teach me to drive a bus?" She leaned toward him, earnest in her request.

"You can already drive a car, I assume."

"Oh, no.... Not yet." She broke a cookie into four pieces and gave one to each of her cats and dogs. "But I'm going to learn."

"Can I go too?" Megan piped up.

"You can go, but only if Daniel says yes."

"Can I, Daddy? Can I go with Jenny on her bus trip to see the world?"

"We'll see...."

Megan made a face. "That means no," she whispered to Jenny.

"Maybe it means maybe," Jenny whispered back.

Daniel smiled as the two of them pressed their heads together, whispering. He'd never been happier.

They ate the last of the cookies and drank the last of the tea, and there was no longer any reason to stay. The party was over. While the children scurried to restore the animals to their rightful places, he stood beside Jenny in the flower garden.

"Thank you for a beautiful afternoon, Jenny."

"You liked it?"

"Yes. Very much." *Too much*.

Her face radiant, Jenny wrapped her arms around him and laid her head on his shoulder.

And Daniel knew he was treading dangerous waters. Standing beside her with her soft hair brushing against his cheek, he wanted to be the one to bring those looks of rosy adoration to her sweet face. Always.

He wanted to be Jenny Love-Townsend's hero.

Somehow he was able to leave the flower garden, though he had no idea how he'd said good-bye. After he'd delivered the children safely to their nanny, he plunged into his work as if all the demons in hell were chasing him.

Long after everybody else had left the Sullivan Enterprise Building, Daniel sat in his office bent over his work, determined to forget an unexpected tea party with a woman who called him wonderful.

THREE

Jenny washed all the teacups except Daniel's. Standing in the kitchen, she ran her finger around the rim. She couldn't bear to wash away the place where his lips had touched.

"Jenny?" Gwendolyn poked her head around the door. "Why don't you leave those dishes till we get back? We don't want to be late for dinner with your folks."

"I'll be ready in a minute."

"Okay, honey. I'll wait for you in the front hall."

Jenny hung the tea towel on the rack to dry, then set Daniel's teacup on a silver tray and carefully carried it upstairs. In her bedroom, she set the tray on a marble-topped table beside a photograph of Jake and Sarah. Then she tenderly lifted the cup and pressed her lips where Daniel's had been.

Closing her eyes, she saw a beautiful vision. She saw herself sitting beside Daniel and his children in a forest glade with all her animals gathered at their feet. The vision was as clear as a photograph pasted into an album, and the caption below it read, *Mr. and Mrs. Sullivan, on their trip to see the world.*

A family of her own. Wouldn't it be lovely?

"Jenny," Gwendolyn called, bringing her back to reality.

Cradling the cup with both hands, she set it on the silver tray, then she positioned the tray just right so that at night she could reach out anytime she wanted to and touch Daniel's cup.

In the doorway, she took one last look at the cup. She loved the way he'd looked drinking his tea, with his eyes all dark and sparkly. Jenny sighed. She'd have to be careful not to dream of too much.

That night Daniel dreamed of Jenny. They were waltzing together in a field of flowers. With her body close to his, she was as graceful as a ballerina. Music swirled round them, and the sun warmed their skin. His hands were hot ... and his body ... The music played on and on, but they were no longer dancing. They were lying together on the flowers, mouths joined, legs and arms twined together. He could taste the heart shape of her mouth. She was sweet, *sweet*. He entered her slowly, and she was sweeter still, so sweet that he cried for her, cried for them both.

He jolted awake. Sweat poured off his face and his body. Swearing, he fought his way out of the tangled sheets and made his way to the bathroom. Leaning against the porcelain, he viewed himself in the mirror. With his wild black hair and eyes, he looked like somebody's worst nightmare come true.

Jenny's. If he didn't rein in his feelings, he was going to be Jenny's worst nightmare come true.

He splashed cold water on his face, then crawled back to bed. He'd failed everybody he ever loved. By all the saints, he would not fail Jenny.

"Miss Gibbs," he said the next afternoon at two-thirty. "I don't like to ask employees to do tasks that aren't in the job description, but I'm afraid I'll have to ask you to take my children to the portrait artist."

"Is that Jenny Love-Townsend?"

"Yes." Would she be waiting in her flower garden with tea she'd made just for him? "Do you know where she lives?"

"Everybody knows where she lives, Mr. Sullivan. She's the town's celebrity . . . the famous painter who is mentally retarded."

"Miss Gibbs . . ." She blanched at the sound of his voice, and Daniel realized he'd practically shouted. He moderated his tone. "You should leave now. You don't want to keep Miss Townsend waiting."

Mentally retarded. His secretary's words hung in the air like a dark cloud. He clutched a pencil so hard, it snapped in two. Daniel flung the pieces into the garbage can, then walked to the window.

Mentally retarded. Labels. How he hated them.

"You're a rebel, Daniel," his father had shouted to him the day they'd put Michael into the ground, the day Daniel had announced he wouldn't be embracing the political career his father had charted for him. "Where is the justice of a God who takes my noble son and leaves the rebellious one behind?"

Labels. How they hurt.

The whole town probably regarded Jenny as retarded, never looking beyond what she was to who she was. By staying away, was he labeling her too?

Muttering dark Irish curses, he strode from his office and stormed through his building, looking for ways to make Sullivan Enterprises the most important corporation in America.

"Jenny was sad," Megan said at dinner that evening.

Daniel wanted to shut his ears to the truth. "You're not eating your chicken, Megan. Eat your chicken."

"Jenny didn't swing with us," Patrick added.

It was a damned conspiracy. Daniel clenched his fists, wadding his perfectly pressed linen napkin into a tight ball.

"She didn't hum, either. And we didn't get to eat cookies and tea. She looked *real sad*, Daddy. How come Jenny was so sad?"

"Sometimes people are sad, Megan."

"Yeah, but how *come?*" His daughter stuck her rebellious little chin out, and Patrick regarded him with solemn eyes.

"I'm not a magician, children. I can't guess the motives of others." But he knew. In his heart he *knew*. "Now eat your dinner."

Dinner was a morose affair. Everybody was relieved when it was over. He sent the children off to play, then, feeling somewhat cowardly, he called the nanny and asked her to come over for the night.

"I have some work to do at the office."

"Certainly. I'm available anytime, Mr. Sullivan."

When Miss Nell Williams bustled in, Daniel felt a sense of order restore itself. Jenny would finish the portrait in a few days, and his life would be back to normal. Until then, he'd keep busy.

Daniel was halfway to his office before he knew he wasn't going there at all. Some dark, destructive impulse made him turn and head across town to a Victorian house with a sign in the yard. He slowed the car, gazing at her house. All the windows were dark. Jenny was sleeping. Perfectly at peace.

But wait. Was that movement at the window? He squinted into the darkness. Not a sign of life. His children had probably been imagining things.

A strange sense of loss haunted him as he turned his car at the end of the street and drove back by Jenny's house, heading to work. The back of his neck tingled. He felt such a strong sense of her presence that he stopped the car in the shadows of a huge oak tree.

Fool, drive on, he told himself, but the eerie sensation of not being alone kept him there.

Out of the corner of his eye, he saw a light come on in a second-story window. Gazing upward, he saw Jenny with her long golden hair flowing over her shoulders.

She lifted a hand, and slowly he got out of the car. The grass cushioned his step as he walked toward the light.

"Daniel?" She'd opened the window and was leaning out, calling softly.

"Jenny." Her name was magic on his lips. He felt as if candles had been lit in his soul.

"I knew you'd come. I kept on my blue dress."

"I just wanted to check on you."

"I'm coming down."

"No . . . wait . . ." he said, but she had disappeared from the window.

What had he done? Gwendolyn was probably going to come tearing out of the house with a shotgun and blow him to kingdom come. And it would be no more than he deserved.

Suddenly Jenny was there, her soft hand touching his.

"Daniel, I'm beside you."

She was more than beside him: She was *in* him, the best part of his heart, an essential part of his spirit. He saw the glimmer of tears on her cheeks.

"You've been crying," he said, touching her cheek. Not since his grandmother had a woman cared enough to cry for him.

"Yes. I thought you had forgotten me."

"I could never forget you, Jenny."

"I'll never forget you, Daniel. Never."

The joy he felt at her simple confession set off alarm bells. Yet he couldn't bring himself to take his hand away from her soft cheek.

"I'm so sorry, Jenny, so sorry I made you cry." He traced her delicate cheekbones and the determined lines of her chin. "I never meant to hurt you."

"I know that."

Her fingers tightened on his, and his right hand lingered on her cheek. They gazed at each other. He got lost in her eyes, and she in his.

"Jenny . . . I don't quite know how to say this . . ."

"Shhh." She put her hand over his lips. He tasted the tips of her fingers with his tongue, just one small taste.

"Be my friend, Daniel," she whispered. "Just be my friend."

Claire had asked for so much, and Jenny asked for so little. Her request honored and humbled him, and in that moment he swore that he would never betray her trust.

"Jenny, I will never hurt you again."

She wrapped her arms around his waist and laid her head on his chest. He curved one arm around her back and one hand around her head. Her silky hair twined through his fingers.

He began to sway, rocking her gently in the cradle of his arms.

"Is this like dancing, Daniel?" she asked, lifting her face to his.

"Almost."

"How lovely it must be."

And Daniel, who hadn't danced in the moonlight in years, began to hum.

"What is that song?"

" 'If I Loved You' from *Carousel*." He bowed at the waist, bending over her hand. "May I have this dance, Miss Jenny Love-Townsend?"

"Why, thank you, kind sir." Her smile was radiant.

She was lithe and graceful in his arms, just as he'd imagined. And he held her close, just as he'd dreamed. With him guiding her, Jenny didn't miss a step. The limp that was so pronounced when she walked was nowhere to be seen, as if the magic of music had made it vanish.

Daniel wanted to lift his voice to the heavens, but mindful of the hour and the sleeping neighbors, he kept his voice low and intimate. For Jenny's ears only.

"I'm dancing," she said, laughing. "Look at me. I feel like Cinderella."

"You should have a thirty-piece orchestra with violins, and a polished floor lit by candles."

"I don't need that. I have you."

Moonlight spilled over them, and summer roses growing beside the front porch scented the air with their perfume. Overhead, the stars lit up the sky.

"Oh, Daniel . . . I could dance forever."

So could he. With Jenny.

They danced on. He went through his repertoire of show tunes, making up words when he forgot the real ones. Somewhere in the distance, a clock tower chimed. Midnight. The hour when coaches turned to pumpkins and dreams turned to ashes.

"I must go, Jenny."

"You'll come back, Daniel?"

"Yes, Jenny. I'll come back."

Standing on tiptoe, she touched her lips to his cheek. "Good night, Daniel."

"Night, Jenny."

She floated across the yard, with her golden hair streaming behind her back. Daniel watched her go, unconsciously holding his hand against the cheek she'd kissed.

"Sweet dreams," he whispered.

Daniel arose for his early-morning jog with a song on his lips. He hummed while he dressed, and it was only while he ate breakfast that he became aware of the song—"If I Loved You."

"It's just a song," he said. Nothing could mar his mood.

Dressed in shorts and a muscle shirt, he raced along his usual route, down the winding driveway of his estate, through the grove of pecans, through the double wrought-iron gates, and down the sidewalk.

Jogging was something he did religiously. A healthy body helped keep a healthy mind, and a sharp mind translated into business success.

He'd built Sullivan Enterprises from scratch, selling discount pots and pans and cosmetics from the back of an old station wagon to housewives on dirt roads. He believed in taking the product to the customer.

"A damned fool notion," his father had said.

But it hadn't been. Sullivan Enterprises now had discount stores on the outskirts of every urban center in the South as well as a thriving mail-order business. Still, Daniel wasn't satisfied. He wanted to make it bigger and better. His immediate goal was to expand to the eastern seaboard.

A couple of bulldogs snapped at his heels as he rounded the corner from his neighborhood and headed down a street filled with brick storefronts, green awnings, and window displays.

A display in the jewelry store caught his eye. Jogging in place, he stopped to look. Behind the glass was a tiny silver carousel, spinning round and round, playing its tinkly tune.

Business expansion along the eastern seaboard was forgotten. Daniel tapped on the glass window.

In his office at the back of the store, the office manager looked up. The store wouldn't be open for hours, but he knew an eager customer when he saw one.

He unlocked the door and let Daniel in.

Gwendolyn still had her nightcap on when the doorbell rang. She hadn't slept worth a flip. Last night it had seemed to her that Bert was under her window serenading her, though her lover had been dead for five years. Probably it was just her hair curlers pinching her head.

Grumbling, she shuffled to the door. Mercy, she was dragging her slippers as if she were an old lady.

She swung open the door, and there stood Daniel Sullivan looking like every woman's dream in tight jeans and open-necked shirt with that wild black hair partially tamed. He was holding on to a silver package for dear life, and he looked as uncomfortable as an eagle at a bluebird party.

"Good morning, Miss Phepps."

"Good morning, Mr. Sullivan." She blocked the doorway with her body. Whatever he was up to, she wasn't going to make it easy.

"Is Jenny home?"

"She's sleeping late."

"I see." He shifted the package from one hand to the other. "I probably should have called first."

"If you want to talk to her about the portrait, you can set up an appointment."

"This is personal."

"How personal?" She was too old for manners and too mean for intimidation. Besides that, she had a sworn duty to protect Jenny. With hands on her hips, she glared at Daniel Sullivan.

Daniel took stock. He didn't want this woman as his enemy.

"Miss Phepps..." He smiled, knowing that sometimes a smile could disarm. "Obviously you have Jenny's interests at heart."

"That's more than I can say for some folks." Arms akimbo, she continued to scowl. She was nobody's pushover.

"I'm going to be perfectly honest with you, Miss Phepps. I drove by last night because my children told me Jenny was sad. She came downstairs and we danced in the moonlight."

"In the front yard?" Things were worse than she had thought. Daniel Sullivan was no ordinary man.

"In the front yard." He was more at ease now. A sign that didn't bode well for Gwendolyn.

"Miss Phepps, I've sworn never to hurt Jenny again. I merely want to be her friend." His face softened. "I know her medical history."

"Do you know her personal history? Do you know how hard she's had to fight for every small victory? Do you know how she struggles to do the things that other people take for granted . . . read the newspaper and write out grocery lists and count out change for a hamburger?" Tears stood in her eyes. "Do you?"

"I didn't know, but I guessed."

"Can you be her friend when she makes a mistake in public, when she stumbles over her own feet or over words? Can you be her friend when people whisper behind her back?"

"I can and I will." Daniel pinned her with his fierce eyes. "Don't deny Jenny a friendship because you underestimate me, Miss Phepps."

A small glimmer of hope sprang to life in her ancient heart. Gwendolyn stepped aside and swung open the door.

"Come in, Mr. Sullivan. You can wait in the sitting room."

"Gwendolyn?" Jenny's voice echoed down the stairs. "Is that Daniel?"

They both turned their faces upward as Jenny descended the stairs. Hanging onto the railing, she tried to hurry, but her feet wouldn't cooperate. Daniel held his breath as she stumbled, then regained her balance. His first instinct was to bound up the stairs and carry her down; his second to let her come under her own power, at her own pace. Jenny had pride. He could see it in the set of her jaw, the tilt of her chin.

She paused at the bottom of the stairs, triumphant, then walked toward him in her tilting, dignified gait.

"Hello, Jenny. You look lovely this morning." She did. Her blouse was the same soft pink as her cheeks. "I hope you don't mind that I dropped by without calling."

"You don't have to call, Daniel. As you can see, I don't have a long line of friends waiting at my door." Her eyes sparkled with humor. "Come into the sitting room."

They went inside, and Daniel firmly closed the door behind them. But Gwendolyn wasn't deterred. In spite of his announced good intentions, she had to see for herself. She went right in behind them.

They were sitting together on the love seat. Too close, was her notion about it all. She plopped herself in a wing chair right across from them.

"Are you comfortable, Miss Phepps?" There was a mischievous spark in Daniel's eyes. Gwendolyn wasn't about to be won over by his easy charm.

"I'm always comfortable, Mr. Sullivan."

"You might want me to move your chair a little closer so you can see better."

"I can see everything I need to from right here, thank you very much."

With his eyes still sparkling, Daniel turned to Jenny. "When I was jogging this morning, I saw something in the window of Jernigan's that reminded me of you." He held out the silver box.

"You bought a gift for me?"

"Especially for you, Jenny."

"I love surprises."

They held the box between them, hands touching. It didn't take a Philadelphia lawyer to see how their hands lingered. Jenny fairly glowed. Any fool could see how she felt about Daniel Sullivan.

And Daniel . . .

He looked so fiercely protective that Gwendolyn was taken aback. Why, he looked as if he was set to go out and slay fire-breathing dragons for Jenny.

Maybe she'd misjudged him.

"It's so pretty, I don't want to open it."

"If you want to keep it wrapped, you can."

"Then I'd never know what was inside."

How they smiled at each other. Gwendolyn had seen smiles like that once . . . on the faces of Jake Townsend and Jenny's mother, Sarah Love.

Jenny's hands trembled on the ribbon, and Daniel steadied them with his own.

"Let me help."

"Yes . . . please."

There was magic in the room, magic between the two on the love seat. Gwendolyn held her breath as they pulled back the silver paper.

"Oh . . ." Jenny put one hand over her heart. "It's too pretty to touch."

What is it? Gwendolyn wanted to say. But she was afraid of breaking the spell.

Daniel reached into the box and took out the most exquisite silver carousel Gwendolyn had ever seen. Holding it gently with one large hand, he wound the spring and the sound of music filled the room.

"Our song," Jenny said.

"Yes. Our song." Daniel set the music box on the coffee table, then stood and bowed over Jenny's hand. "Shall we dance?"

They danced together as if they'd been born to do so, while strains of music filled the room . . . "If I Loved You."

Gwendolyn got up quietly and left the room, shutting the door behind her. The sounds of music and laughter echoed faintly in the hall.

It almost made her believe in miracles. She

left the hallway and went into the kitchen, humming.

Behind the closed door, with Jenny in his arms, Daniel felt ten feet tall. He'd given her a small trinket, and she'd given him unconditional adoration. He'd come out the winner.

The music box wound down, and they collapsed on the love seat, laughing.

"Oh, my, Daniel." She put her hand over her heart. "If I'm going to dance so much, I'll have to take up jogging to get into shape."

"I jog every morning. Do you want to jog with me?"

"I'm slow."

"I need to slow down."

"Oh . . ." Her cheeks glowed with pleasure. "You really want me to jog with you?"

"Yes. I really do." It was the truth. "Everything I do is a solitary pursuit. I'll enjoy your company."

"Can we go early and see the sunrise?"

"Yes. It's my favorite time of day."

"Any time of day with you is my favorite, Daniel." Jenny touched his face.

Daniel's heart stood still. *A friendship*, he'd told Gwendolyn. To even consider anything more would be devastating . . . to both of them.

Her hand lingered, trembled.

A friendship. That's all it could ever be.

"We'll be jogging partners." He took her hands and cradled them in his. "I'll see you tomorrow, Jenny."

"Until tomorrow," she whispered.

He left her sitting on the love seat, holding the music box next to her heart.

Until tomorrow, Jenny.

FOUR

Jenny didn't have to set her clock. Sheer excitement propelled her out of bed and down the stairs. When Daniel came, she was waiting on the front porch.

He looked like a hero coming through her gate. A song her mother used to sing echoed in her mind, "Someday My Prince Will Come." Her prince was coming up the sidewalk dressed in jogging shorts, and she felt like Cinderella.

The only difference was, Cinderella had an enchantment that changed her from a raggedy cinder girl to a beautiful princess. There was no such enchantment for Jenny. She would always be trapped inside a body that didn't cooperate and a mind that couldn't communicate.

Sometimes she longed to be different. Times like now. She longed to be able to race down the

A Prince for Jenny

steps without tripping and to say something so clever that Daniel would be astonished at her wit. She longed to have a house she lived in all by herself and her own car so she could go zipping about town visiting friends who would always be glad to see her. And she longed—oh, how she longed!—to be the kind of woman who would make men proud to be seen in her company.

But then, if she were different, she wouldn't be Jenny, and she wouldn't have Jake and Sarah and Gwendolyn and her brothers and sister. But most of all, she might not have Daniel.

She smiled at him, and he smiled right back. Her heart seemed to grow bigger, and she wondered if that's how love felt to normal people.

"Good morning," Daniel said, leaning on the porch railing.

She searched her mind for something clever to say and the right words to say it, but in the end she could only speak from her heart.

"I'm so glad to see you, you take my breath away."

"I don't know that I've ever taken anybody's breath away."

"Do you mind?"

"No." He smiled again. "It's a fine way to start the morning."

"Good. I'll tell you every morning how you take my breath away."

She loved the way he laughed. It was a deep, rich sound that was better than music. When he took her hand and helped her down the steps, she felt as if she might fly instead of jog.

"I thought we'd jog in your neighborhood in case you get tired. If I go too fast, tell me."

"Okay."

"Hold tight, Jenny. Don't let go."

She wouldn't have let go if wild elephants had been stampeding her.

The morning air was fresh and sweet and full of birdsong. She'd never seen the grass look so green, the sky so blue. Always, with her artist's eye, she'd seen things other people didn't. But seeing with the heart added yet another dimension.

"Oh . . . look," she said, pointing to a cardinal winging upward. "He's like a flame against the sky."

She got so caught up in watching the cardinal that she forgot to concentrate on her feet. They betrayed her, and she felt herself going down.

"Oops." Daniel put his arm around her waist and caught her to his chest.

"Those cracked sidewalks can be treacherous," he said, gallantly excusing her clumsiness. He held her close, gazing at her with such tenderness, she wanted to stay on the sidewalk forever.

She wondered if it was possible to die of happiness.

He leaned so close, she could feel his warm breath against her cheek. Even the air around them seemed to tremble as his lips almost touched hers.

Almost.

Jenny closed her eyes, afraid to look a miracle in the face.

"Let's rest," he said, abruptly pulling back and leaning against the trunk of an oak tree.

She pressed her hands tightly together, wishing, wishing with all her might to be normal.

"I'm too slow for you, Daniel."

"Ah . . . Jenny."

The sadness in his voice broke her heart, and she came dangerously close to feeling self-pity. She balled her hands into fists and jutted out her chin.

"Don't you ever feel sorry for me, Daniel Sullivan."

"Jenny, it's not pity I'm feeling. It's something far more dangerous."

They stared at each other, trapped in two separate worlds, while the sun topped the eastern horizon and spread its splendor across the sky. Slowly Daniel reached for her hand.

"It's time to go back, Jenny."

It would always be time to go back for Jenny.

She was silent as he led her back down the sidewalk, silent as he led her through the gate and up the porch steps.

"Good-bye, Jenny," he said, bending down to kiss her cheek.

"Good-bye, Daniel." She waved as he started down the walk. "Come again."

At the gate he turned for one last look, and she knew he might never come again.

Daniel stood rigid under the cold shower.

"Fool. Imbecile. Idiot."

He had almost kissed her. Standing on the sidewalk with her sweet face turned up to his, he'd come within a hair's breadth of crushing her lips under his, of caressing her slim back, of fitting his hard body into her delicious curves. He'd wanted her. Not in any sedate, friendly way, but desperately, the way a passionate man wants a desirable woman.

Scowling fiercely, he turned his face upward to the blast of cold water. By all the saints in heaven, what was he going to do about Jenny?

He was still scowling when he arrived at Sullivan Enterprises.

"Miss Gibbs," he snapped. "Come inside for dictation. We have a hard day's work ahead."

"Yes, sir." She all but saluted. Employees bent on pleasing. That's what he liked. Order. Purpose. Success.

Was Jenny in her flower garden, painting?

"Take a letter to Michael Gravlee.... Dear Mike, My offer to buy Gravlee Discount Stores still holds...."

Was Jenny dancing in the sunshine while the carousel music box played their song?

He balled his hand into a fist and banged it onto the top of his desk. Miss Gibbs nearly jumped out of her skin.

"Sir? Did I do something wrong?"

"It's not you, Miss Gibbs. It's me."

Helen Gibbs stared at him, stricken. Then she leaned forward and asked softly, "Is there anything I can do to help you?"

Compassion wasn't in her job description; she was offering it freely ... and it felt good. Perhaps he'd been wrong all these years, pursuing his career with such single-minded obsession that there was room for nothing else. Success was sweeter with a human element. Even Claire had known that.

"Will you accept my apology, Helen?" Daniel left his chair and offered his hand.

"You called me Helen." Flabbergasted, she

barely touched his hand, then sank back into her chair.

"We've been working together for ten years. It's about time, don't you think?" He gave her a lopsided grin.

"Yes, sir, Mr. Sullivan."

"Call me Daniel." That felt good too. Informality. Compassion.

Perhaps he had a real heart after all.

Jenny's music box sat on the silver tray beside Daniel's teacup, playing it's tinkly tune.

"Daniel," she whispered, and her heart swelled with the beauty and the pain of loving him.

If she were an ordinary woman, she would tell him so, and he would love her right back.

An ordinary woman.

She walked across the room with her lurching gait and stood before the mirror. Except for her limp, she looked just like anybody else. If she didn't know better, she might even fool herself.

But she couldn't fool Daniel. She squeezed her eyes shut, remembering how close his lips had come to hers. So close, he'd almost kissed her. Almost.

Tears squeezed from under her lids and rolled down her cheeks. Daniel would never kiss her.

A Prince for Jenny

She was wishing for too much. Gwendolyn had warned her, but she hadn't listened.

Jenny went into the bathroom and washed the tears off her face. Daniel would never come again. In her heart she knew it was true. In her heart she also understood how he would suffer, making the decision to stay away.

She didn't want him to suffer.

She blew her nose and scrubbed her cheeks one last time, then sat on the edge of her bed and picked up the telephone and dialed information.

Long ago she'd learned it was easier for her to ask a faceless operator than try to look up numbers in the telephone book. Daniel's business number. Would he answer?

Her knuckles turned white as she squeezed the phone and listened to it ring.

"Daniel Sullivan."

Overcome by surprise and delight, Jenny cradled the phone next to her ear and sat there smiling.

"Daniel Sullivan," he said again.

Goose bumps rose on her arms.

"This is Jenny."

"Jenny?"

He sounded glad to hear from her. Or was she dreaming?

"Daniel, I can't paint today because I feel a dark cloud in my heart and my work won't be good." She spoke all in a rush before she changed her mind. *I love you, Daniel*, she wanted to say. *I love you enough to set you free.*

"Are you okay, Jenny?"

"I don't feel sunshine in my soul, but it will come back."

"I'm so sorry . . ." She held on to the receiver, listening to the wonderful sound of his breathing. "I wish I could put the sunshine in your soul, Jenny."

"I do, too, Daniel." Oh, how she wished he would.

They both held tightly to their telephones, wishing for things that could never be. Their hearts yearned across the great distance that separated them, and even the silence seemed to mourn.

"Is there anything I can do to help you, Jenny?"

"Nothing . . . Thank you."

"You'll call when you feel like painting again."

"Gwendolyn will."

"Of course."

"Good-bye, Daniel."

"Good-bye, Jenny."

She couldn't bear to break the connection first. Long after she heard his receiver click into place, she sat on the bed hugging the telephone to her chest.

A Prince for Jenny

Daniel replaced the receiver, but he couldn't bear to relinquish Jenny. He sat in his chair absently running his fingers over the smooth surface of the telephone as if that small action would bind her to him.

"Jenny... Jenny," he whispered.

Did she sense his real feelings? Was she frightened of him? He'd rather die than have Jenny afraid of him.

He shoved his chair back and was halfway across the room when he realized that his impulse to go to her and explain was self-serving.

She'd called to cancel. Her message was clear: stay away.

Daniel was off the hook.

Funny. He didn't feel off the hook. He felt heartsick.

He paced the room, trying to make sense of what was happening to him... and to Jenny. Always, he'd been hopelessly inept in matters of the heart.

He punched the intercom. "Helen, would you come in here for dictation."

Work. That was the thing.

"Liar, liar, pants on fire," Jenny whispered.

She'd lied to Daniel. He was the only person

in the world who could help her. Not her mother or her daddy or her brothers or her sister or Gwendolyn. Only Daniel.

She sat at her desk, took up her drawing pencil, and sketched his face. Then she drew a circle of hearts around his image.

"I love you, Daniel."

Clutching the drawing close to her chest, she remembered the first time she'd ever loved another person besides her mother. Jake Townsend. How she loved Jake. And how she had fought to have him in her life.

Other memories came, ancient memories.

"Jenny might never walk," she heard the doctor tell her mother.

Oh, how she had struggled to prove the doctor wrong.

"She might never talk," he'd said.

And she'd given the graduation address at Vanderbilt when her brother and her sister had received their degrees.

Suddenly Jenny knew what she had to do. Anything worth having was worth the struggle. Jenny tipped up her chin and left her bedroom. In the hallway she could hear Gwendolyn's snores. Poor Gwendolyn, worn out from worrying over her. No wonder she needed an afternoon nap.

Quietly Jenny made her way down the stairs,

holding on to the railing so she wouldn't stumble and make a racket. In the kitchen she packed a picnic basket, then sat at the table and wrote a note. *Dear Gwendolyn* . . . She chewed her bottom lip as she wrote, determined to spell everything just right. *I borowed your car. I hope you don't minde. Jenny.*

Humming to herself, she took the basket and Gwendolyn's car keys, then climbed behind the wheel of an aging Buick and sat there smiling.

Oh, she could picture herself racing down the street. All alone. Driving.

She took a deep breath and inserted the key. Nothing happened. Jenny furrowed her brow, trying to remember what her brother Josh had told her so many years ago.

Turn the key.

She was rewarded with the purring of the engine. Exhilarated, Jenny put the car into gear and stepped on the gas. She shot backward at a wonderful speedy clip, mowing over a hydrangea bush in full bloom and plowing down the birdbath.

"Whoops." Now, how could she get the car to go forward? She was threatening the corner of the garage when she finally figured it out.

Shoot, there was nothing to this driving. Now that she knew the gears, she could certainly keep it on the road.

Triumphant, she roared out of the driveway. Loud crashing noises heralded her progress. Looking in the rearview mirror, she saw the mailbox standing at a crazy angle and a little sapling wearing the same paint as the car.

Would Gwendolyn be upset about that? If the car lost a little paint, Jenny would replace it. She was an expert at paints. Maybe she'd paint flowers and rainbows on the car.

She couldn't think about that now: What she had to think about was how she would ever find Daniel.

Gwendolyn clutched the note in one hand and hung on to the back of the chair with the other. Jake Townsend hovered near the doorway like a thundercloud.

"If I hadn't slept the afternoon away like some silly old fool, none of this would have happened."

"Stop blaming yourself, Gwendolyn. It's not your fault."

"If anything happens to her . . ."

"Nothing is going to happen to her. I won't let it."

Age had mellowed him. He still had the look of a fierce old hawk, but his voice was quieter, gentler. Sarah's influence. Gwendolyn had known from the moment she met Sarah Love that she was the only woman who could tame Jake.

Just having him in the house made Gwendolyn feel better. She sank into the chair, still holding the note.

"I guess I should have told you about Daniel Sullivan sooner."

"You don't know that's why she left."

"Yes, I do, Jake." Gwendolyn spoke with quiet conviction.

And suddenly Jake knew too. Memories stirred. He'd been sitting on Sarah's front porch swing beside four-year-old Jenny. She'd laid her tiny cheek against his chest and murmured, over and over, "Me love 'ake. Me love 'ake."

When Jenny loved, she loved with her whole heart, and nothing would ever convince her to give up.

"I'm going to find her, Gwendolyn."

"Good luck, Jake."

He'd need more than luck when he found her: He'd need the wisdom of Solomon.

The commotion on the street brought Daniel to his feet. He sprang to his window, with Helen not far behind.

Car horns were honking, crowds were gathering, and people were screaming. The center of all the excitement was an ancient Buick, driving sedately up the sidewalk. All four fenders were dented, the tailpipe banged the concrete, and the front bumper swayed like a drunken sailor. A clothesline filled with somebody's laundry trailed behind the car, and the radio antenna sported a rakish flag—a pair of bright red undershorts.

"Who in the world . . . ?" Helen said.

Behind the wheel sat a laughing imp with a lopsided bow in her hair.

"Jenny." Astonishment and delight filled Daniel. And hot on their heels came fear, absolute terror that Jenny had been behind the wheel of a car.

He raced from his office and down the stairs, two at a time.

"Jenny!" he yelled as he catapulted through the front door.

The car was stopped on the sidewalk, with smoke pouring from the hood. Out stepped Jenny. When she saw him, she strolled forward in her brave rolling gait, holding a picnic basket with one hand and her hair bow in place with the other.

"Daniel. I drove the car." Her smile was triumphant and her cheeks were flushed.

"You certainly did." He couldn't bear to chastise her for taking to the streets in a car she obviously didn't know how to handle. She was safe, and that was all that mattered.

The old car backfired once, then with a mighty sigh it sank into its warped frame and died.

Daniel caught Jenny and held her close. "You certainly did drive the car." Pride welled up in him, and feelings so tender, he dared not give them a name.

Jenny tipped her head back and smiled at him. "Now will you teach me to drive a bus?"

Daniel roared with laughter. Then, taking her by the elbow, he led her to the elevator. She leaned against the wall and pressed one hand over her heart.

"What a ride! I've never had as much fun in all my life."

"It was your first time driving, I take it."

"My second. My brother Josh tried to teach me years ago, but Daddy decided it wasn't such a good idea."

"I expect there are a few housewives in Florence who would agree with him."

"I didn't mean to take their laundry. It just happened."

"Jenny . . . Jenny." Daniel caught her hand, smiling. "What are we going to do about all that missing laundry?"

"Tie it up with a ribbon and send it back?" She gave him a hopeful, pert little smile.

"I'll have Helen do just that."

"Good. I don't want to be a thief."

She got off the elevator and walked beside him, swinging her picnic basket and humming. She was a thief, all right, for she had completely stolen his heart.

When he walked into his office, Helen was sitting at her desk as if the commotion underneath the window had never taken place. Daniel put a protective arm around Jenny. She was her usual unaffected, charming self, and Helen was gracious. If she hadn't been, if she'd shown any indication that she considered Jenny *mentally retarded*, Daniel would have fired her on the spot.

"Helen, I'd like you to see that the laundry on Jenny's car is returned to its rightful owner."

"Certainly." Helen was as unflappable as if he'd asked her to bring up the mail.

"With a ribbon," Jenny said.

"Any particular color?"

"Yellow."

"Send flowers, too, Helen," he added.

"What shall I say on the card?"

"Jenny?" Daniel turned to her.

"Say 'I'm sorry I took your laundry. Come by and I'll paint your portrait free.' "

"Florence is a small town. It shouldn't take you long to find who's missing a clothesline. Also, call Gwendolyn to let her know Jenny is safe, and when you've finished delivering the laundry, take the rest of the day off. Jenny and I are going to have a picnic."

To her credit, Helen acted as if he had picnics in his office every day. "I hope you have a lovely time," she said, closing the door behind her.

Alone with Jenny, Daniel suddenly felt shy.

What could he say to this wonderful, innocent woman who had brought sunshine into his life? He wanted desperately to be her hero, to be compassionate and strong and noble. But most of all, he wanted to be wise.

He took the picnic basket, then gently held both her hands. She had her brave little chin tipped up, and she was smiling at him as if he were the most wonderful man in the world.

"Jenny . . ." She had risked her life to see him. He had to stop speaking and clear his throat.

Jenny pressed her fingertips over his lips.

"I love you, Daniel." Her face was earnest and her eyes shining. He trembled at the simplicity and the power of her confession . . . and all it meant to both of them. "Is it all right if I pretend we will someday live together happily ever after?"

Was it? Was he wise enough to let her dream without giving her false hope?

She folded her hands tightly together and waited for his answer.

"Yes, Jenny. It's all right."

"You don't have to love me back. I know I'm slow."

"You're not slow, Jenny, you're different in the way that flowers are different, and trees and birds. They come in all colors and varieties, and each one is special." He unlaced her hands and lifted them to his lips. Such talented, beautiful hands. "And I do love you, Jenny . . . in the way that one good friend loves another."

Liar. He loved her in ways that would terrify her if she knew.

"Then you're not mad that I came."

"No. I'm touched and humbled by your courage. You're the most courageous person I know, Jenny."

She gave him a wicked little grin. "No, I'm not. I took Gwendolyn's car without asking. Do you think she'll be mad?"

"We'll face the music together. I'll go with you and explain to her that this dangerous and noble mission you undertook required just the right car. And if it's a little worse for wear, I'll be glad to pay for the necessary repairs."

She stood on tiptoe and kissed his cheek. "Daniel, I love you so much, my heart hurts."

His heart hurt too. It was shattered by a love that was totally impossible.

He put his hand on her cheek, stealing a

moment of softness and tenderness, storing it away in his memory so he could take it out late at night when the loneliness closed in around him and threatened to destroy his soul.

Don't love me too much, Jenny. I don't know how long I can be strong if you love me too much.

"Why don't we see if there's anything in that picnic basket that will cure a hurting heart," he said, trying to keep the mood light.

"Will we picnic here?"

"Where would you like to picnic?"

"By the river, under a great big tree."

"Then a river you shall have. And the biggest tree in Florence, Alabama."

Daniel took the basket with one hand and Jenny with the other. Heads turned when he left the building.

Can you be her friend when people whisper behind your back? Gwendolyn had asked. No one at Sullivan Enterprises dared whisper behind his back.

FIVE

He was going to take Jenny picnicking in the large, safe company car, but when she saw his Thunderbird convertible, she was enchanted.

"It looks like a doll's car." She walked round and round it, running her hand across the bright blue paint.

"Would you like to ride in that one?"

"Is it yours?"

"It's all mine."

"Oh, Daniel, what fun!"

He'd never known a woman who took such great delight from such simple pleasure. She leaned back in the seat with her face turned up to the sun and her hair blowing in the wind. On the bridge over the Tennessee River, her hair ribbon pulled loosed and floated toward the water. Even that made her laugh.

"When I have a car of my own, it will be like this, with no top."

The longing in her voice ripped at Daniel's heart. Could Jenny ever have a car of her own? Was it possible for someone like her to get a driver's license? He realized how little he actually knew about her condition. What were her capabilities? Her limitations?

The first thing he was going to do after this picnic was find out.

"Would you like to drive, Jenny?"

"Drive? Me?" She put both hands over her heart, and her eyes were luminous with joy. "You'd let me drive this magical car?"

"Yes. We'll go to a remote country road, and I'll give you a lesson."

"Daniel, you're the most wonderful man in the world."

The road was so remote, it didn't even have pavement, let alone traffic. Jenny gripped the wheel so hard that her knuckles turned white. She understood everything Daniel was telling her, but could she make it all come out right?

She had to. She *would*.

"Ready, Jenny?"

He was smiling and completely relaxed. Daniel trusted her.

"Ready." She took a deep breath as she reached for the gear shift. *Do it with confidence*.

"You'll be fine, Jenny." He put his hand over hers. "I'm right here beside you."

She eased into gear and tapped the gas pedal. The car crawled forward.

"It's okay to go faster, Jenny. If we go off the road, we'll drive around in the pasture for a while. We might even reach out the window and pick a bouquet of wildflowers."

Joy. She could go fast. She rammed her foot down harder. The car shot forward, but she kept it on the road.

"Look at me, Daniel. I'm really driving."

"You're really driving, Jenny, and doing a hell of a job too."

She accelerated some more. The wind sang in her ears and whipped her hair.

"Yep. I'm doing one hell of a job." She laughed with the sheer wonder of it all. "Whoops... Daniel. The curve."

"Turn the car..." She spun the wheel. "The other way... that's right." He sat there as calmly as if she were one of those great racecar drivers she'd seen on television.

"I could drive forever."

"You can drive as long as you want."

"Well, almost forever. I'm getting hungry."

"Then let's find that tree you talked about."

Daniel found the biggest tree beside the river. It was a mammoth hundred-year-old oak with strong spreading branches that provided shade for them and shelter for a family of gray squirrels and a large collection of birds. Jenny noted each tree dweller with wonder and delight. The Tennessee River, rolling along at the base of the bluff and singing its timeless song, was a special source of joy for her. Even the dappled patterns of sunlight and shadow underneath the tree delighted her.

Daniel realized that the thing he loved most about Jenny was that she didn't view the world as ordinary mortals did: She saw with her heart. In fashioning her, God had filtered out the darkness—the violence, the hatred, the jealousy—and left only the light. Jenny's light touched even the lowliest creature and transformed it to a thing of beauty.

With her, Daniel felt the greening and blooming of his soul.

He knelt at her feet and took her hand. "Teach me, Jenny. Teach me to see with my heart."

"You already see with your heart, Daniel. . . . You saw me." She touched his chest, then pointed to her own.

"You're the best thing that's ever happened to me, Jenny."

"Truly?"

"Truly."

At that precise moment, a shaft of sunlight pierced the thick branches and touched Jenny's hair and her face. Crowned with gold, she looked as if she had come from another world, his beautiful innocent princess.

His feelings for her were so powerful that they went beyond love, so powerful that they would not be denied. Neither the saints in heaven nor the hounds of hell could have kept him from touching her face.

Her skin was soft, silky, her face perfectly fashioned for the shape of his cupped hands. Joy filled him, threatened to overflow.

Unconsciously Jenny's tongue flicked out and wet her lips. *Dew on rose petals.* With one finger he gently traced the heart shape of her mouth.

A small sigh escaped her, and she closed her eyes. She was so close, so sweet. Daniel was tempted almost beyond endurance. He leaned down until his lips were only a whisper away from hers. The scent of flowers clung to her skin and wafted from her hair.

One small taste. That's all he'd take. One small, sweet devastating taste of her tempting lips.

Jenny's lids fluttered open, and she held Daniel in silent, solemn regard. Spellbound, breathless, they watched each other... and waited.

There was not a sound, not even the whisper of flight as a cardinal left the tree branch and winged his way upward. One of his feathers floated downward and landed in Jenny's lap. It lay against her white skirt like a scarlet accusation.

Like a man waking from a dream, Daniel slowly released Jenny. What had he been thinking of? He'd almost defiled an angel.

"Daniel... I thought you were going to kiss me."

"I almost did, Jenny. I apologize."

"Please don't apologize." Jenny thought her heart would break. "I understand."

"It's not that I don't want to kiss you..."

"You *want* to kiss me?"

"Yes. I've wanted to from the first moment I saw you."

She could hardly believe what she was hearing. Daniel wanted to kiss her. Joy flooded her soul, and hard on its heels, sadness.

"I understand. Truly I do." She picked up the lovely scarlet feather and held it to her cheek. It was her consolation prize. "I just wish..." She let her voice trail off. Gwendolyn used to say, *If wishes were horses, beggars would ride.*

"You wish what, Jenny?"

"Sometimes I wish I could have one kiss . . . a small one . . . so I'd know what it's like."

"You've never been kissed?"

"Do kisses from family count?"

"No."

"Then, no . . . never."

Daniel's hands trembled as he cupped her face.

"Just a small kiss, Jenny . . . between friends."

"What joy, Daniel!"

Her eyes were luminous and so blue that, bending closer, he felt as if he had been sucked into their center. He felt the whisper of her warm breath against his cheek and the stirring of her silky hair against his fingertips. Her lips were close now, soft and innocent, so very innocent.

His mouth closed over hers slowly, tenderly. *God*, he prayed. *God, give me strength to kiss her once, then turn away*.

She put her arms around his neck and drew him closer. When her lips moved under his, sweet and sure, he knew that a just God had given womanly instincts even to Jenny, His special child.

Light exploded through him, and a feeling of such exquisite joy that he felt the tears wet upon his face. Every nerve ending in his body tingled. He wanted to deepen the kiss, to plunge his tongue into the warm, moist recesses of her mouth and taste her fully, completely. He wanted to ease his ache by fitting her body close to his. He wanted to feel the sweet heat between her thighs and to know the tender swelling of her breasts.

Beast that he was, he wanted to lower her to the ground and teach her the ways of a man and a woman. He could almost feel the satin sheath of her virgin flesh as it closed around him. The agony of wanting her and knowing he could never have her was so great that he cried out.

Alarmed, Jenny pulled back.

"Daniel, did I do something wrong?"

He pulled her into her arms and cradled her tenderly against his chest.

"No, Jenny . . ." *My darling . . . my love.* "You did everything right. You're perfect."

Sighing, she leaned against him.

"I didn't know kissing would feel like falling," she said.

"Did you feel as if you were falling?"

"Yes. Part of the time. Then I felt as if I were flying." She tipped her head back so she could look into his eyes. "My heart flew, Daniel."

"So did mine."

She traced his mouth with her fingertips. Daniel felt as if he'd been touched by angels.

"The day I first saw you, I dreamed about kissing these lips. . . . You've made my dreams come true, Daniel."

How could he tell her that she'd made his come true as well? How could he tell her without raising impossible hopes?

Jenny. Jenny.

The feel of her hands upon his lips sank into his very soul. Such a tender touch. He would remember it always, remember and cherish. Pulling her into the circle of his arms, he held her close. She leaned her head against his shoulder and wrapped her arms around his waist.

Her trust was both blessing and burden. He didn't know if he had the strength to endure it.

"Daniel . . ." Jenny pulled back and grinned up at him in an impish way. "Do you want to chase sunbeams?"

"I've never chased sunbeams."

"I'll teach you." She took his hand and led him into the sunlight. "Do you want to sneak up on them, or do you want to be bold?"

"Let's be bold, Jenny."

They raced about, reaching up toward the sunlight, laughing as the sunbeams touched their hands, then filtered through their fingers. Daniel had not known such a carefree moment since he was a boy.

"I almost got one, Jenny." He held his hands out, cupped, to show her how he had almost trapped the sunshine.

"Try with your tongue . . . like this." Jenny

stuck her tongue out and tipped her face toward the sun. "Hmmm, delicious."

"Save one for me."

With the sunlight beating down upon his face and Jenny at his side laughing, Daniel felt as if he'd slipped backward into a time before the existence of evil. He was the first man, with Jenny as his Eve, and this happy place beside the river was their Garden of Eden.

"I wish I never had to leave," Jenny said when they were too tired to chase any more sunbeams and were packing the remains of their picnic into the basket.

"We'll have many picnics, Jenny."

"Truly?"

"Truly," he said, really believing they would.

He drove home slowly, stopping once to purchase a peace offering for Gwendolyn. She was waiting for them on the front porch, her face bunched up with worry.

"Jenny!" She lumbered down the porch steps and wrapped Jenny in her large embrace. "Thank heavens you're safe." She scowled at Daniel.

"Didn't Helen call you?" he asked.

"Yes . . . Jenny, honey, why don't you take the picnic basket inside?"

" 'Bye, Daniel." Jenny put her hand briefly on his cheek. *A touch of heaven.* "Thank you . . . for everything." A lovely blush colored her cheeks.

Daniel could hardly bear to let her go. He took her hand and caressed the long, slim fingers. "I'll never forget today, Jenny."

Gwendolyn cleared her throat loudly to show what she thought of their leave-taking.

Jenny gave him a conspirator's grin, and he winked at her. When she carried her picnic basket into the house, she was humming.

Gwendolyn waited until the sound of Jenny's voice faded before she had her say.

"Your message came too late. When I woke up and found her missing, I called Jake and he nearly went wild. It wasn't until after he left that I saw the message light on the answering machine."

The situation was Daniel's worst nightmare come true.

"You've every right to be angry. I should have brought her home first to make certain that no one would be worried."

"First?"

"If looks could kill, I'd be dead."

"Wait till Jake Townsend gets through with you."

"Gwendolyn, I'm not the enemy. I would never do anything to hurt Jenny." Suddenly, remembering the peace offering, he held it out.

Gwendolyn looked at the hat. It was one she'd always wanted, a genuine Panama, handwoven in

Ecuador, the kind she could wear in Florida when she retired and had nothing to do but lie in the sun all day like a sausage, frying herself.

"I won't be taking bribes," she said.

"It's not a bribe; it's a gift." He laid the hat on the front porch.

"I won't be wearing it." Her fire suddenly gone, Gwendolyn sank into the rocking chair and wiped a tear from her eye with the hem of her painter's shirt.

"When you brought her that music box and I saw the two of you together . . ." She heaved a big sigh, then wiped another tear. "Oh, Lordy, I don't know what to believe anymore."

Daniel knelt beside her on the wooden porch floor and took her hands. "I want what's best for her too. Trust me, Gwendolyn."

"Sometimes I want to." She shook her hands loose from his, then gave him a wry grin. "Lordy, how you do turn an old woman's head. No wonder Jenny's in love with you."

Daniel walked to the edge of the porch, leaned against the railing, and studied the front yard. Flowers of every kind were in bloom, and the trees were alive with birdsong. Such a peaceful place. A haven for Jenny. What right did he have to disrupt her life?

"You know that, don't you, Daniel?"

"Yes."

"How are you going to handle it?"

It was a question he'd wrestled with almost from the moment he'd met her.

He turned back to Gwendolyn. "I honestly don't know."

The old porch floor creaked as Gwendolyn left the rocking chair and came to stand beside him. "Maybe you ought to find out." Her face softened as she reached up to pat his cheek. Then she drew herself up and scowled at him. "And don't you be thinking I'm a soft touch, because I'm tough as an old bulldog and twice as mean." She marched toward the front door, then came back to pick up her hat. "And don't you think I'm fixing to wear this hat."

"I wouldn't dream of such a thing."

"Good."

Daniel let her have the last word, then got into his car and drove back to Sullivan Enterprises. Although it was thirty minutes after closing time, the lights were still on in his office.

Upstairs, Helen met him at the door.

"I thought I told you to take the rest of the day off."

"You have a visitor."

He didn't have to be told; he knew. "Jake Townsend?" Helen nodded, too awestruck to do more. "Where is he?"

"In your office. I told him I didn't know

if you'd be back, but he said you would, said something about having written the book on obsession. I didn't dare tell him the offices closed at five." Her hands fluttered anxiously over the top of her desk. Finally she latched onto her steno pad and clutched it to her chest. "Shall I go in with you?"

"No, Helen. Go home. I'll handle this alone." She gathered her purse and her umbrella. Rain or shine, Helen always carried an umbrella. At the door, she turned for one last look. Daniel smiled at her. "Thank you, Helen. You did the right thing."

The door closed behind her, and Daniel squared his shoulders. It was time to face Jake Townsend. He knew how the biblical Daniel must have felt when he faced the den of lions.

SIX

Jake Townsend was a great lion of a man, as tall as Daniel himself and just as erect. He had a thick mane of hair that had once been very black but now had enough silver to be called salt-and-pepper, and his eyes were a pale, clear and riveting green. He didn't say a word when Daniel walked in, but leaned back in his chair and treated Daniel to the most intense scrutiny he'd ever endured.

Do I pass inspection? he might have said to someone else, but he didn't dare say it to this man.

"Daniel Sullivan," Jake said. It was not a question.

"Yes." He offered his hand, and Jake took it. His handclasp was strong and firm. "Helen told me you were waiting. Can I get you a cup of coffee?"

"No, thank you. This is not a social call."

Daniel sat in his desk chair, hoping the act of sitting behind his own desk in his own company would give him an advantage. It didn't. In Jake Townsend, he'd meet his match.

"Before you say anything, Mr. Townsend, let me assure you that Jenny is completely unharmed."

"I expected nothing less of you." Jake leaned forward and fixed him with a piercing stare. "A Vietnam hero, medevac pilot, flew rescue missions over Da Nang and Chu Lai. Daring Danny Boy they called you, Savior of the Wounded."

Daniel gripped the armrests of his chair. He'd been so young, too young to know fear. It all came back to him, the steamy jungles, the screaming of the wounded, the blood running like rivers.

"Got one more for you, Danny...."

The popping noises in the distance might have been mistaken for firecrackers celebrating another Fourth of July if it hadn't been for the bodies that were loaded aboard his helicopter. Gnats swarmed in with the wounded.

"Too late for this one, the poor bastard...."

His dogtag was barely visible in the tattered remains of his shirt. Sullivan, Michael, Captain, U.S. Army.

Too late. Too late for his own brother. Oh, God... His hands froze on the controls.

"Get out of here, Danny. NOW!"

Daniel took a deep, steadying breath. The past was behind him—Vietnam, Michael, his father, Claire. All the people he'd failed. The important thing was not to fail again, not to fail Megan and Patrick . . . and Jenny.

He left his desk and poured himself a cup of coffee.

Jake made a careful steeple of his hands, never taking his eyes off Daniel. "There was never any doubt in my mind that my daughter was safe *from* you and *with* you. The thing that bothers me most is that in her present state of mind she is not safe from herself."

"The car." Restless, Daniel remained standing.

"Precisely. Call me overprotective, call me any damned thing you like, but I will not allow Jenny to be put in jeopardy again as she was today."

Lesser men might have been intimidated by Jake Townsend, but Daniel had one advantage over lesser men. He loved Jenny as much as Jake did. Perhaps more, if that was possible.

"I agree that taking the car was a dangerous thing for her to do, but she did a remarkable job, considering that no one ever taught her to drive." It was a subtle criticism. Daniel watched to see how Jake would react.

"You have children."

"Yes . . . two."

"Then you know what it's like to want to keep them safe from all harm. I lost my first wife and daughter in a car accident . . . I owe my happiness, my very life, to Jenny and her mother, and I would gladly give mine for them."

"As I would for mine."

"Megan and Patrick, ages eight and five." Jake gave him what passed for a smile, one father to another. Under different circumstances they might have been great friends.

"The first thing I did when I left Gwendolyn was to check up on you," Jake added. "There's not much about you that I don't know."

"There's one thing about me that you don't know." Daniel put his untouched cup of coffee back beside the coffeepot, then returned to his chair behind the desk. Taking a pencil in his hands, he faced Jake. "I love Jenny."

The silence in the room was so complete, it appeared that neither man even breathed. As Jake and Daniel sized each other up, the only sign of turmoil was the twitch in Jake's jaw and the way Daniel clenched his pencil. It finally gave way under the pressure. The small popping sound brought them out of their trance.

"Everybody loves Jenny. She's an easy person to love."

Jake's statement gave Daniel a temporary reprieve from his ill-timed confession. He loved Jenny. The knowledge sang through him like a symphony. He'd loved her from the moment he'd first seen her swinging in her backyard. Need, desire, passion. He'd called his feelings all those things. But the simple, wondrous fact was that he loved her . . . man to woman, prince to princess, Adam to Eve . . . loved her enough to let her go.

"Yes, she's an easy person to love," Daniel said, and in that moment he knew he'd betrayed her. Coward. Bastard. The self-recriminations would have to wait; now he needed all his energy focused on the powerful man sitting in his office.

"I had hoped . . ." Too proud to continue, Jake bowed his head as his heart broke for Jenny. What had he expected from a virile, powerful, intelligent young man? Daniel Sullivan would never declare a romantic interest in a woman like Jenny. He'd choose someone who was his equal in every way, someone who could give him children.

Jake straightened his shoulders and fixed Daniel with a steady gaze. "Know this about Jenny: When she loves, she loves with her whole heart. I can't change the way she feels about you, but I can help her forget."

Cold winds swept across Daniel's soul. He'd lost her, lost her because he had neither the courage nor the wisdom to claim a special woman as his own.

"Sarah and I will take her on a long trip... she loves to travel." Jake didn't have to say more. His eyes said it all. *Unless you love my daughter enough to claim her, stay away.*

Jake stood up. The interview was over.

They didn't shake hands; they merely parted, not as enemies but as two men who shared a common goal—protecting Jenny.

Daniel stood alone at the window, staring out into the darkness as he mourned the loss of a woman who had taught him to taste sunbeams.

SEVEN

The cake wasn't turning out exactly the way Megan wanted it to. She frowned at the cookbook, then scowled at her brother. Everything might have been all right if she hadn't let him put in the eggs.

"How did I know you was s'posed to take 'em out of the shell?" he said.

If only he wouldn't cry, she'd send him out of the kitchen and make the cake all by herself.

"Besides, you shoulda asked Miss Williams," Patrick added.

"Miss Williams is a nanny. She's not a cook. And besides, I want to surprise Daddy."

"How come he's sad?"

" 'Cause grownups get that way sometimes, silly. Now hush talking so I can think."

She wished she knew about fractions and stuff,

but she didn't guess it took a mathematical genius to figure out how much sugar to put in a cake. Lots and lots.

"This is going to be delicious," she said, smiling.

The open letter lay on the table beside Daniel's chair. He didn't have to look at it to know what it said.

Dear Daniel, I have to go away on a trip. It wont be a bus trip like I planned, but it will be nise. Don't forget me. Forever yours, Jenny.

As if he could ever forget her. He lowered his head to his hands.

"Jenny," he whispered. "Jenny."

"Surprise!"

His two children stood in the doorway looking like two survivors of a kitchen war. Chocolate decorated their faces, their hands, and the fronts of their clothes, and flour billowed from them like mushroom clouds. Between them they held a dilapidated creation.

"We made you a birthday cake, Daddy," Megan said.

Daniel almost said, "It's not my birthday," but seeing their radiant faces, he stopped himself.

"That's wonderful, Megan . . . Patrick. Let's see it."

Grinning from ear to ear, they blazed a white trail across the carpet. The thing they called a cake was great chunks of sticky dough held together with toothpicks and hope. Gobs of chocolate sat in fat random patches around the platter. Strawberries formed a crude D; small colored candies made a smiley face, and on top of it all were six twelve-inch candles from the candelabrum on the dining room table.

Daniel was grateful they hadn't decided to light the candles.

"Hmmm. It makes me feel hungry just to look at it." Heedless of their condition, he set the cake on the table, then hugged his children close. "I'm so proud of you."

"Honest?" Megan asked. "Cross your heart and hope to die?"

"Honest. Cross my heart and hope to die." They plastered his face with chocolate-flavored kisses, then he set them on their feet. "Shall we go into the kitchen and eat this wonderful cake?"

They skipped along beside him, chattering a blue streak. For a few blessed minutes he forgot the letter beside his chair.

Jenny knew it was foolish to keep watching out the window. Daniel wasn't going to come.

But, oh, how she hoped he would. Clutching the curtain in one hand and pressing the other against the windowpane, she imagined Daniel riding up on a white horse like a knight in shining armor and rescuing her.

Sighing, she let the curtain swing back into place. How silly she was. Wanting to be rescued from flying off in a private jet with a family who loved her. How ungrateful.

Her suitcase was open on the bed. She took a pink blouse from its hanger in the closet and folded it carefully. Then slowly she walked to her suitcase.

"Are you about finished, Jenny?" Gwendolyn called from the hallway.

"Not quite." She had barely started.

"We'll leave for your parents' house as soon as you finish packing."

Jenny wondered if she could take two weeks. Maybe if she took two weeks, Daniel would come for her.

She took the pink blouse out, unfolded it, and put it back on the hanger. She was tired of wearing pink.

Outside her window a mockingbird called. Jenny's left leg dragged more than usual as she made her way back to the window.

Daniel carried Jenny's letter in his coat pocket. When he least expected it, the words flashed into his mind, obscuring everything else. *I have to go away.... Don't forget me.*

"Daniel?" His secretary's voice brought him back to the matter at hand. Dictation.

"Where was I, Helen?"

" 'I will be in North Carolina'..."

"Ah, yes." Daniel leaned back in his chair. "... 'for the grand opening'..." It would be a party. How Jenny would love a party. "Take a break, Helen."

"But the letter..."

"Can wait."

Helen gathered her steno pad and stood up. "Are you feeling all right, Daniel? You haven't been yourself lately. Maybe you should take some time off."

"I'm fine, Helen. Just tired, that's all."

When the door closed behind her, he took the letter from his coat pocket and read it again. Jenny was leaving. She would be chasing sunbeams without him, and seeing sunsets and moonlight and stars, all without him. An aching sense of loss almost overwhelmed him.

Moving like a tired old man, Daniel picked up his desk calendar and scanned his notations. Expansion to the East Coast complete. Opening gala being planned. Inquiries from the Midwest about putting his stores there.

He was succeeding beyond his wildest dreams. Then why did he feel so empty?

Jenny. Always Jenny.

Daniel closed his eyes and pressed his hands against his lids as if the pressure could drive her from his mind. But even if she left his mind, he knew that she would never leave his heart.

Impossible, he'd said about loving Jenny. And yet, until he met her, "impossible" was not even in his vocabulary. All his life he'd defied convention, had done the unthinkable as well as the impossible.

How could he dismiss the possibility of loving Jenny in every way without knowing the facts? Hope sprang to life in him, and such joy, he almost shouted.

He buzzed for Helen to come back inside. Before she was even seated, he was firing off the rest of the letter to North Carolina.

"Let's see . . . where was I? . . . 'for the grand opening on July 15. My secretary will call you when all travel arrangements are complete. Regards,' etc." Daniel was pacing now, fired up with a new purpose. "After you get that letter off, cancel all my appointments for the rest of the day. We have some sleuthing to do."

It took them exactly one hour to find out

what Daniel wanted to know. When he left the office, he was whistling.

Dr. Wayne Dodge didn't usually see people on such short notice, but he was intrigued by the man and by the request. He pushed the thick glasses that were always sliding off his nose back into place so he could see the man better. A fine figure of a man, he was. More than handsome. He had character in his face. Wayne Dodge prided himself on always being able to judge whether a man had character.

"So, Mr. Sullivan . . . you want to know about Jenny Love-Townsend?"

"I don't expect you to reveal privileged information about her medical history, I merely want to know what she is capable of."

"And the nature of your interest?"

There it was. The big question. When Jake had asked, Daniel had equivocated. Never again would he betray Jenny.

"I love her, Dr. Dodge, but as her father pointed out, most people do. I'm *in love* with her."

Wayne Dodge had to pull off his glasses to wipe the moisture from his eyes. When he put them back on, he was smiling.

"Jenny Love-Townsend has been my patient

since she was four years old. I will tell you this, she's bright. She processes information perfectly. She understands *everything*."

Daniel leaned back in his chair. Jenny *understood*. Innocent as she was, she still had the same dreams and longings as an ordinary woman.

"The problem with Jenny is that there is a short circuit somewhere. Her intake is perfect; her output is imperfect. She's not Down's syndrome as you know it; that's why her looks fool you. We don't know why she's special. Lord knows, Jake Townsend has carried her to medical experts all over the world."

"Could she get a driver's license?"

"Certainly." Wayne Dodge laughed. "But over Jake Townsend's dead body."

"He's unusually protective of her."

"Diplomatically put." Wayne Dodge removed his glasses once more and began to polish them. "I'm speaking now strictly as a friend of the family. After Jake married Sarah, he gave Jenny every advantage that money could buy, the best schools, the best doctors. He took her everywhere... the ballet, the symphony, the theater, New York, Paris. She's always had this amazing artistic talent. Jake saw that she studied with the best artists in the world. All strictly chaperoned, of course."

"Gwendolyn?"

"Yes. She'd been Jake's executive assistant for years. When Jenny turned sixteen, Gwendolyn's sole duty was to chaperone and protect Jenny."

"Sort of an old-fashioned duenna."

"Again, aptly put." Dr. Dodge laughed. "You have to understand Jake's background to know why he was so protective with Jenny, particularly why he never let her drive a car. . . . You see, his first wife and daughter were killed in a car wreck. He blamed himself because he was driving."

"You've been more than helpful, Dr. Dodge; you've made me a very happy man."

"If you're made of the kind of stuff I think you are, you'll make Jenny a very happy young woman. But I'm warning you, don't expect life with a special woman to be easy."

"Nothing worth having is ever easy."

Daniel went straight to a telephone booth on the corner. He'd wasted too much time already. He was so excited that he dropped the telephone book twice before he found Jenny's number. Then he put his money in and dialed.

The phone rang . . . and rang . . . and rang . . .

"Blast it all," Gwendolyn muttered. The phone was ringing again. Probably somebody

A Prince for Jenny

wanting a portrait done. If she answered it, they would *never* get to Jake and Sarah's house.

"Jenny . . . honey . . ." She stuck her head into Jenny's room. Jenny was staring out the window, and her suitcase was on the bed only half packed. "I can help you pack if you'd like."

"No, thank you."

Downstairs the phone was still ringing. Well, let it ring.

It stopped as Gwendolyn lumbered down the stairs, then it started up again. Whoever it was didn't give up easily.

She started to pass it by and go on with her tea making. A cup of tea. That's what she needed. Some crazy impulse made her pick it up.

"Hello?"

"Gwendolyn . . . this is Daniel Sullivan."

This was bad news. Gwendolyn sank into the Queen Anne chair beside the telephone table.

"Thank God you haven't left," he said.

Or maybe it was good news. Gwendolyn put her hand over her heart. She was going to tell Jake she couldn't do this job anymore; then she was going to go down to Florida and find that little retirement cottage she'd been dreaming about.

"Is Jenny there?"

"What do you want with her?"

"If she's there, I want to come over and see her."

"We're on our way out of the house. I'll give her a message."

"What I have to say is too important to say over the phone."

Gwendolyn didn't know what to do. If she told him no, she might be destroying Jenny's only chance for the kind of future other young women took for granted. If she told him yes and things didn't work out right, Jenny would be completely destroyed. It was a no-win situation.

"Don't let her leave," Daniel said. The decision was out of her hands. "Are you there, Gwendolyn?"

"I'm here."

"I'll be there in fifteen minutes. Please keep her there that long . . . Gwendolyn?"

"I want to believe this can work."

"I'll make it work."

"Jake should know."

"I'll make it right with Jake later, Gwendolyn. Right now the most important person is Jenny. Please . . . give her this chance. Give me this chance."

Upstairs, Jenny would still be staring out the window, waiting and hoping and dreaming.

"Daniel, how can I say no?"

"Anything you want is yours, Gwendolyn. Name it."

"There is one thing . . ." Gwendolyn had a

vision of Jenny as a small child climbing into her lap with a book so dog-eared and jelly-smeared, the words were barely discernible. But it wasn't the words that thrilled Jenny; it was the pictures. She'd punch her favorite picture with an emphatic little gesture, then point to her chest. "P'ince. *My* p'ince."

Gwendolyn told him what she wanted. After she'd hung up, she prayed that Daniel Sullivan would be Jenny's prince.

She put her sketch pad in the suitcase, and her pencils. The packing was almost done.

Jenny drifted to the window once more. Hopeless. Gwendolyn had warned her to know the difference between a dream and reality. Everybody had warned her.

The curtain slid back into place, and she started to turn from the window. That's when she saw the horse, a white horse of all things, coming down the street. Enchanted, Jenny opened the sash and leaned her elbows on the windowsill. The rider was dressed in some kind of costume, shiny black boots and red-lined cape. It must be some kind of parade.

But where were the bands?

The horse was coming at a gallop, his hooves clattering on the pavement. His rider cut a dashing figure as he lifted himself from the saddle and waved his hat. It was a plumed hat, and the feather was bright red.

"Jenny!" The horseman knew her name. "Jenny!" he called again, waving his hat.

Jenny's hand flew to her heart. It couldn't be. Horse and rider came closer, close enough to see. It was Daniel with his dark hair and fierce eyes and beautiful lips. Daniel, her hero. Daniel, her prince.

"I'm here," she called, leaning out the window and waving.

He brought his mount to a halt underneath her window. His hat was in one hand, and in the other a bouquet, Queen Anne's lace and black-eyed Susans and honeysuckle, all the wildflowers they'd seen the day she'd driven his car and chased sunbeams and received her first kiss.

"I know you are, sweet Jenny. That's why I came." He held up the flowers. "Bearing gifts."

"I'm coming down." Jenny raced down the stairs, stumbling and crying and humming all at the same time. "Gwendolyn!" she called. "Gwendolyn! He's here! He came for me!"

Gwendolyn peeped out the window and saw Daniel on the white horse. "Saints be praised," she said.

The front door banged behind Jenny, and

suddenly she was standing on the edge of the porch with her arms outstretched.

Daniel leaned out of the saddle and scooped her up. With his arms holding her tight, he kissed her, kissed her without her having to ask, kissed her in the front yard for all the neighbors to see.

At that moment Jenny believed in miracles.

"I love you, Jenny." He cupped her face. "Do you hear me, Jenny? I love you with my heart and soul. I love you the way a man loves a woman, and if you'll let me, I'd like to show my love."

Jenny trembled inside, but she kept her eyes open, watching Daniel. She was no longer afraid to look a miracle in the face.

"I want to eat in fine restaurants with you and dance in public places with you. I want us to go to movies and the theater and skating rinks and bowling alleys and parks together. I want to court you, if you'll say yes. . . . Say yes, Jenny."

"Yes. Oh, Daniel . . . yes, yes, yes!"

Let other women run without falling. Let them be the belle of the ball with their wit and their charm and their sophisticated ways. Jenny had Daniel, and she now knew what it meant to be special.

EIGHT

Daniel rediscovered simple pleasures—strolling down the street with Jenny, holding hands and eating ice cream from a cone; whispering at the back of the theater when the movie was so bad, it was funny; sitting on a front porch swing with Megan and Patrick piled on top of them, singing crazy songs and laughing.

He rediscovered magic.

And Jenny discovered a craving for independence.

"I have a plan, Gwendolyn."

They were in the kitchen having an early morning cup of coffee. One look at the stubborn set of Jenny's jaw told Gwendolyn all she needed to know: Jenny's plan was likely to get them all in trouble.

"Do I want to hear this?"

"Of course you do. You're part of it."

"That's what I was afraid of." Gwendolyn took a fortifying drink of coffee. She figured she'd need it. "So . . . are you going to tell me or what?"

"You're my friend, Gwendolyn. My best friend in the whole world."

Gwendolyn knew she was a goner. When Jenny got that twinkle in her eye and that sweet cajoling smile on her face, nobody could deny her anything.

"Bribery won't work on me, you know."

"I know. Daniel does too."

Gwendolyn snorted. Daniel Sullivan knew no such thing. Nearly every time he came through the front door, he was carrying an armload of gifts. All that candy was making her fat as a pig, and she was going to tell him so one of these days. Maybe. If she ever figured out a way to do it without hurting his feelings.

She did love that French perfume he'd brought. And the gold bracelet. And the soaking tub for her feet. Especially the soaking tub.

"I'm not saying I like any of it," she said.

Jenny laughed. Then she went to the window

and looked at Gwendolyn's car sitting in the driveway, all its dented fenders and sagging parts repaired.

Someday she was going to get herself a car. But first things first. She turned back to face Gwendolyn.

"I'm going to get a driver's license, and you're going to help me."

"The saints preserve us."

Gwendolyn wore her Panama hat to interview the young man who agreed to teach Jenny the fine points of driving.

"Can you keep a secret?"

"Yes, ma'am. I can do anything you ask. I need the money." The oldest of nine children, Jay Potter was trying to work his way through college and out of poverty.

"This is going to be a surprise for a few people we know." Daniel for one, Jake for another. He was going to be blustery as a March wind, but he'd get over it. "And if it doesn't work out, I'm not about to have people saying that Jenny failed. She's as smart as can be in spite of everything, and I don't want you to ever make her feel any different." Gwendolyn gave him a fierce stare. "Do you understand."

"Oh, yes, ma'am."

"Good. Then when do we start?"
"How about tomorrow?"

They took to the back country roads for fear of discovery. Farmers on tractors plowing their red clay fields became accustomed to the sight of the lanky rawboned youth, the motherly matron in her Panama hat, and the lovely young woman with the lopsided bow in her hair.

After three weeks of intensive training, Jay and Gwendolyn declared Jenny ready for her driver's test.

Jenny was scared, but she wasn't about to let it show. Young men and women, mostly high school age, bent over their driver's tests, yellow pencils clutched in their hands. Such confidence they had. And such careless disregard for their ability to scan the questions and quickly mark the answers.

She felt a stab of envy, but it passed as quickly as it came. How could she, who had so much to be thankful for, feel envy for people she didn't even know?

"Are you ready, Miss Love-Townsend?"

The kind-faced man who spoke would take her to a private room and administer her test verbally.

"I'm ready."

Suddenly she was no longer scared; she was proud. She'd done it. She'd done what most people thought she couldn't do.

On a balmy night in late June, Daniel returned from work and saw Gwendolyn's car in his yard. Jenny! Something had happened to Jenny.

His heart racing, he ran into his house, expecting the worst. What he saw was Jenny and his children covered with flour and chocolate and smiles. Megan and Patrick stood on chairs on either side of her, and between them was a large mixing bowl. They were up to their elbows in flour.

"Surprise!" Jenny's face was wreathed in smiles. "I drove, Daniel, with a license I earned all by myself." Her grin turned impish. "On the sly."

"I'm in love with a devious woman." Heedless of the flour on her apron and the chocolate on her cheek, he hugged her close. "I'm proud of you, Jenny."

"Am I debious, too, Daddy?" Patrick tugged on his sleeve.

Daniel scooped him into his arms. "You certainly are . . . in here making surprises for Daddy." Jenny took a batch of cookies from the oven. "Umm, they smell delicious."

"Daddy." Patrick cupped Daniel's face with his flour-smeared hands. "I like Jenny."

"So do I, Patrick."

"Can she be my mommy?"

All the heartbreak of a small motherless boy was in his voice. Megan came to Daniel and wrapped her arms around his hips.

"Can she, Daddy?" Megan asked.

He'd thought of nothing else for the last month. Leaving Jenny each night on her own doorstep was agony. Going to separate beds was torture. He'd kept telling himself it was time . . . time to talk to the children, time to talk to Jenny.

Courtship was one thing, but marriage was altogether different. Courting Jenny, he could give her all the things she'd missed, a ride in the moonlight in an open car, lazy picnics by the river, and sweet embraces under the shade of the trees, flowers and music boxes and bonbons. He could show his love in a hundred different ways. And he had.

But it wasn't enough. He'd known from the beginning that it would never be enough.

He'd handled courtship with a special woman. But was he wise enough to handle a marriage?

The silence in the kitchen was complete. Jenny watched him with wide blue eyes and deliciously rounded mouth. Color bloomed in her cheeks and one hand was pressed over her heart.

His eyes never left hers as he held on to his children. So much was riding on his answer; so many lives depended on him.

"Jenny, it seems my children have preempted me. I wanted to propose with candlelight and music and roses. I wanted to take you someplace special and give you a very special ring." Such love shone on her face that he wanted to take her into his arm. But not yet. Jenny had to have her chance to choose.

"All of us love you very much, Jenny, and we would like for you to be an official part of our family. But we know that marriage is a grave responsibility, and if you'd rather just be our friend, we'll understand. In either case we want you in our lives."

"Daniel . . . I don't need roses and candlelight and music. I don't need special places and a special ring." Because of her great emotional turmoil, her speech was more halting than usual. "I will be honored to be a part of this family."

Slowly she came to them, came with all the grace and dignity that was Jenny. And because she saw with her heart, saw their greater fear and their greater need, she hugged the children first. She took Patrick from Daniel's arms, then knelt so Megan could cuddle close.

"You're my dream come true . . . the children of my heart." She gently pressed her palm over their small chests, then pressed it over her own. "I will take care of you and love you always and forever."

Do you dream? Jenny had once asked, and he'd been ashamed to tell her no. Kneeling, Daniel wrapped Jenny and the children in his arms. She'd given him back his dreams.

Love swelled through him like a river, full of power and brightness and promise, and he swore he would never let them go. Never.

When Jenny awoke the next morning, a bright blue Thunderbird convertible was sitting in her driveway. And around it was an enormous red ribbon. She threw on her robe and hurried to her front porch.

Daniel and Gwendolyn were sitting in rocking chairs drinking coffee and smiling like two Cheshire cats. And on Gwendolyn's head was the genuine Panama hat, the one she'd sworn she would never wear.

"We thought you were never going to wake up," Gwendolyn said. "This man of yours has come bearing gifts again." She patted the hat on her head. "I've been wanting one of these for years... for when I go to Florida. I don't know how Daniel knew."

Jenny did. She'd told him.

"Because he's magic," Jenny said, smiling at him. He winked. Secrets. She loved having secrets with Daniel. "Why is your car wearing a ribbon, Daniel?"

"Because it's not my car . . . it's yours."

Gwendolyn was so excited, she could hardly sit still.

"It's an engagement present, Jenny, and guess what else he's got." Jenny and Daniel both burst into laughter. "Well, if I'm all that funny, I'll go into comedy and get rich instead of sitting here in a rocker like an old lady and wasting my time with the two of you."

"I don't think Daniel and I would be very good at comedy, Gwendolyn."

"Humph. Who asked you to go?"

"If you go, we'll have to go," Daniel said seriously. "We can't live without you."

"Bosh!" Gwendolyn waved them away, but her face was pink with pleasure. "Are you going to sit here all day and devil me, or are you going to show her the ring?"

Daniel smiled. It seemed he and Jenny were destined to share all their private moments with someone else. But he didn't mind. In fact, he loved it. His summer with Jenny had taught him that the greatest pleasure of all was in sharing your life with people you love.

Reaching into his pocket, he pulled out a

red velvet box. It was so old, the nap had worn away on the edges. He lifted the lid, and inside lay a delicate filigreed ring. The antique gold had a pinkish cast, and intertwined among the filigreed hearts and roses were diamonds, rubies, and pearls.

"A special ring for a special woman." He slipped the ring on Jenny's finger. It was a perfect fit. "It belonged to my grandmother, Molly Sullivan. She would have approved of you, Jenny. She would have loved you."

"It's the most beautiful ring in the world. I will cherish it, always."

"I think I'm going to cry," Gwendolyn said. And she did.

"It's more than a ring, Jenny; it's a symbol of our love. I want the whole world to know that I've chosen you."

MILLIONAIRE ENTREPRENEUR TO WED DOWN'S SYNDROME WOMAN. The headlines screamed at Daniel.

He jerked the newspaper off the bed and glared at the item in the society pages.

Daniel Sullivan, self-made millionaire, is set to wed a well-known artist with Down's syndrome. Jenny Love-Townsend is famous in her own right. Portrait artist to presidents and kings, she took the eye of Sullivan this summer while she was doing a portrait of his two children. Sullivan and his fiancée are in Raleigh this week for the opening gala of yet another Sullivan Store.

The reporter had done his homework well. There was a recent photo of Jenny, taken when she'd been a guest at the White House, and one of him ducking into a limousine in Alexandria, Virginia, where he'd gone to visit his father.

Daniel ripped the front page off the paper and threw it into the wastebasket. He wanted nothing to destroy the weekend for Jenny. It was their first outing together away from Florence, away from the people who had watched Jenny grow up and who were proud of her success. Kind, caring people who made her feel loved.

He fastened the last stud in his tuxedo shirt. It wasn't too late to cancel. He could call Ed Cranston, the new store's manager, with some excuse. He and Jenny could fly out before anybody got a chance to question her about the newspaper article.

There was a soft knock on the connecting doors.

"Daniel . . . may I come in?"

Although the door wasn't latched, he opened it for her. She took his breath away. He'd never seen Jenny in anything except the filmy dresses she was so fond of wearing or a pair of old shorts or old blue jeans. Now she was dressed in a form-fitting sequined gown the same shade of blue as her eyes.

"I'm dazzled, Jenny."

"So am I." She touched the onyx studs on his shirt. "You look like a prince." She smiled at him almost shyly. "My prince."

If he lived to be a hundred, he would never cease to be grateful to her for that one special gift: She always made him feel like a hero.

"And you're my princess."

"Truly?"

"Truly."

"I'm a little nervous."

He folded her into his arms, fitting her tightly against his chest. "We don't have to go," he whispered into her hair. "All I have to do is alert my pilot, and we can be home in a couple of hours."

"And miss the party?"

"Yes. Who needs a party when I have you?" The wadded-up newspaper accused him from the wastebasket.

"It will be my first party with you, Daniel." She slipped her arm through his and smiled up at him. "I want to be frazzled." Her brow furrowed. "Dazzled," she amended, smiling.

Jenny, my sweet Jenny. He'd destroy the first person who made an unkind remark to her.

"Let me get my coat," he said.

The reception room was enormous, and filled with people in fancy dress.

"Look, Daniel. They must have picked every flower in North Carolina."

"It looks that way." He had one arm around her waist, and that's where he intended to keep it. "Stick close beside me . . . I don't want you to get lost."

"You could never lose me."

Ed Cranston saw them and came forward with a woman he introduced as his wife. They both stared at Jenny, but neither made any reference to the engagement or to the newspaper article.

So far so good. Daniel would make a quick round of the room, press a few hands, then whisk Jenny away.

Another group of people spied them and came by for small talk. Although some of them were frankly curious and didn't try to hide their stares, they were cordial.

"What a wonderful party." Jenny said after they left. "My feet are not used to these tall shoes. If I rest in this chair a minute, will you get me something cool to drink?"

How could he refuse her? As he made slow progress he glanced back every now and then at Jenny. She smiled and waved at him.

Just as he reached a table laden with food, he saw a couple approach Jenny. She smiled warmly at them, and they smiled back. Then they started talking.

Her animation gradually faded and the color drained from her cheeks. He wanted to tackle everybody in his way, then grab Jenny and run.

A silent scream of anguish tore Daniel's throat. Helpless, he could do nothing except watch from the other side of the room.

"When we saw the newspaper this morning, we were so excited." The woman whose name she could no longer remember was standing too close. Her strong perfume smothered Jenny. "I said to George, 'George, we're going to get to meet that handicapped woman that paints.'"

"Yes, I paint." George was leaning down staring at her as if she were a fish in a bowl. Jenny searched the crowd for Daniel. Where was he?

"And imagine, going to marry a millionaire," the woman said.

"I guess it takes all kinds," George said.

"Shush, George. If it suits them, it suits me." She punched Jenny's arm. "Right, hon? I mean, Lordy mercy, how many retarded women get to marry a millionaire? You must be doing something right, hon."

The room began to spin. Jenny clutched the sides of her chair. She would *not* make a scene. She would not embarrass Daniel that way. Nor would she embarrass herself.

She stood up slowly and was pleased to see that she was at least four inches taller than the woman.

"Will you excuse me, please?"

"Sure, hon." The woman punched her arm again. "By the way, that was a pretty picture in the paper."

"Thanks." Her mother had taught her to be polite.

Jenny stumbled as she turned to go. Now, that would make a lovely picture for the paper. Retarded woman embarrasses her fiancé by falling on the floor.

She caught her balance on the back of a chair and walked on. The hateful voices followed her.

" . . . couldn't tell a thing by looking at her."

"Maybe that's how she fooled him. Though with that body of hers, I don't guess he cares what her mind is like."

Jenny fought the urge to cover her ears. People called to her as she hurried through the crowd. A few hands reached out to her. She ignored them all. She had to get away.

A Prince for Jenny

The ladies' room loomed just ahead, and she knew her guardian angel was on duty. She pushed open the heavy door and sank onto the velvet-covered setee. If she didn't put her head between her legs, she was going to be sick.

As she bent over she saw the two newspapers on the table beside her chair—*The Raleigh Journal* and the *Carolina Tattler*. She saw the words DOWN'S SYNDROME in bold print and ran her finger along the headline. MILLIONAIRE ENTREPRENEUR TO WED DOWN'S SYNDROME WOMAN. She was not just a woman; she was a Down's syndrome woman. The other was not so kind: RETARDED WOMAN SNAGS MILLIONAIRE.

"Daniel, what have they done to you?"

She started reading the *Carolina Tattler*, frowning as she followed the words with her fingers. Disgusted, she flung the paper down. It would take her forever to decipher all the hurtful words. And what good would it do?

Retarded woman snags millionaire. They were calling her retarded. And she hadn't even known Daniel was a millionaire. Didn't even care. Daniel was Daniel. She loved him for himself.

But why did he love her?

She buried her face in her hands. The antique ring had turned upside down on her finger and bit into her cheek. Slowly she lowered her hands.

Daniel *did* love her. The ring was proof. His kindness was proof.

Oh, he was the dearest man in all the world, and here she was sitting in the bathroom ruining his party. She reapplied her lipstick, then straightened her shoulders and stuck out her chin.

Nobody was going to ruin Daniel's party.

Daniel saw her coming, the color back in her cheeks and her chin held high. He felt like weeping and cheering at the same time.

"There you are," he said, trying to disguise his relief.

"I ran away, but now I'm back."

In that simple sentence she told him everything he needed to know. They'd crucified Jenny, and she'd emerged triumphant.

"You don't ever have to run away, Jenny. You're the best, the *very* best."

Daniel, who had never been given to public displays, leaned down and kissed her. A flashbulb popped.

Another reason to protect her, he thought.

Another reason to be brave, she thought.

"Have you had enough of this mad crowd?" He kept his arm securely around her.

"Yes." She would be glad to leave. Nothing in her life had prepared her for this kind of censure.

She'd led a sheltered life. Jake and Sarah had seen to it.

Suddenly she saw the couple who had made the unkind remarks. Unconsciously, she squeezed Daniel's arm.

"Jenny?" He took one look at her face, then began to search the crowd. When he saw the couple, his face turned grim with rage. "You don't have to see them or their like, ever again." The crowd parted as he hurried her toward the door.

She had a vision of how the rest of her life would be: hiding in bathrooms while Daniel fought her battles.

"Wait." Her chin came up. "I want to stay."

"Are you sure?"

"Yes. And I want to send a note to that couple."

She dug into her evening bag and pulled out pencil and paper, the tools of an artist. She was never without them. Daniel found a chair for her, and she did her sketch quickly. The writing took a while longer.

When she finished, she handed it to him.

"Please check the spelling. I don't want to embarrass myself at your party."

Daniel read the note first; it was simple and sincere, like the woman who wrote it. *Daniel chose me becuse he sees with his heart.* The drawing was a cartoon, more telling than words. She had drawn herself in a swing with her skirt touching the ground. He was kneeling beside her, holding her hand, and on the front of his shirt was an oversized heart. Around them she'd sketched people with accusing eyes and scowling faces.

He took her pencil and quietly changed the spelling of "because." Then he knelt beside her and took her hand.

"You are the most remarkable woman I've ever met, Jenny Love-Townsend, and I'll always be honored to be seen with you at my side."

Her smile was typically Jenny, innocent, sweet, and endearing. On the way to deliver the note, he stopped to ask Ed Cranston the names of the couple and what their positions were in Sullivan Stores.

"Maxine and George Roderick. She doesn't work for me, but he's my senior accountant."

"Find another one," Daniel said.

The Rodericks practically kissed his feet when he arrived with Jenny's note.

"I have two messages for you. This is from my fiancée." He handed the note to George Roderick. "The other one will be in your box on Monday morning." He left them with their mouths hanging open. "Shall we go now?" he asked when he returned to Jenny.

"Now we can go."

Standing outside her bedroom door, he gathered her into his arms. "This is the best part of my day," he whispered before his lips descended on hers.

He was gentle with her, sweet, and she loved every minute of it. But lately she'd felt how he was holding back. The muscles in his upper arms were tightly corded and his neck and back were stiff.

He was even careful to pull his hips back as soon as she began to feel the wonderful, mysterious changes in his lower body.

"Good night, my love," he whispered.

"Good night, Daniel."

Already bruised from her encounter at the party, she felt a crushing sense of defeat when he handed her into her room and shut the door. She leaned against it, listening to his footsteps in the hall. She could hear when his door opened, hear when he entered the room next door.

Didn't he want her the way a man wanted a woman? Gwendolyn had told her how it would be... under duress, of course. And Jenny had felt all that swollen flesh.

She remembered Gwendolyn's exact words. *Sweaty, tangled coupling.* Why couldn't she have the sweaty, tangled coupling?

Jenny undressed and put on her gown. The changes in her body were evident. Her breasts were fuller, heavier, the nipples puckered and hard. And oh, that sweet heat between her thighs. It was wonderful and terrible at the same time. And it happened every time Daniel kissed her.

So many of her dreams had come true, was she selfish to be dreaming of more?

Her mind swung back to the party. Had her dream become Daniel's nightmare?

Jenny knew of only one thing to do, and that was find out the truth. Without design or forethought, she pushed opened the connecting door.

"Daniel?"

He was standing beside the window with his back to the door. Every nerve in his body tensed when he heard her call his name. He turned slowly, and the sight of her made him catch his breath.

She couldn't have looked more desirable if she'd planned a midnight seduction. Her hair was loose and disheveled, her white cotton gown hung off one shoulder, and her cheeks were pink with excitement.

Desire slammed into him so hard, he almost reeled.

"I'm glad I didn't wake you," she said.

"You didn't." Sleep was the furthest thing from his mind. Standing there clad in nothing but his shorts and his passion, he was grateful for the darkness.

She came straight to the window, wrapped her arms around his waist, and laid her head on his chest. He bit back a groan.

Easing his hips sideways, he put his arm around her shoulders. Her thin gown was no protection. His skin felt seared where her body touched his.

"Having a restless night, Jenny?" Was that desire-clogged croak his voice?

"Yes."

No matter what was happening in his life, he could count on Jenny to cut right to the heart of the matter. One of the hallmarks of the truly innocent was total honesty.

Daniel thought of the news article resting in his wastebasket. Where did you draw the line between being protective and being dishonest?

Jenny held on a moment longer, then stepped out of his embrace. "I know about the newspaper stories. Did you know?"

"Yes . . . I wanted to spare you that."

"I don't want to be protected." She squeezed her hands tightly together, praying for the right words. "I'm no longer a child. I'm a woman."

"There was never any doubt in my mind that you're a woman, Jenny."

"Would you have told a normal woman?"

Would he? Would they have laughed together over bad press, or would his male ego have demanded that he play the role of protector and hero?

"I honestly don't know, Jenny."

"Would a normal woman be sleeping in a separate bedroom?"

Caught off guard by her sudden veering of topic, Daniel couldn't come up with a quick answer. The truth was, he would definitely *not* be sleeping in a separate bedroom. But how could he say that without hurting her? Another truth was that he loved Jenny more than he'd ever loved another woman. And yet, because she was special, he felt an urgent need to protect her . . . even from himself.

His silence damned him.

Jenny put her hands over her face, then balled them into fists and began to pace. He'd never seen this defiant side of Jenny, and he'd never loved her more. She was magnificent, stalking about in the moonlight with her filmy gown swirling around her lovely legs and defining her high, proud breasts.

"I want truth and pain and real emotions . . . I want to sleep in the same bed with you, Daniel, and to know *everything*." Only inches away, she stood in front of him, tall and beautiful and so desirable that she took his breath away. Her chin came up and her eyes shot sparks. "I don't want to be treated like a *retarded* woman."

Fierce and swift, he closed the space between them and pulled her hard against his chest. Pressed full against her, he felt every tempting curve and every sweet hollow in her body.

"I never meant to do that, Jenny. Never."

"Do you want to love me, Daniel . . . man to woman?"

"More than you can possibly know."

"I know, Daniel." To his astonishment and delight, she touched his rigid flesh. It was a fleeting touch, so butterfly soft, he might have imagined it. "Gwendolyn told me."

Her eyes were so big and blue and innocent that a man could get lost in them.

"Jenny . . ." He was determined to be strong, but her slender fingers touched him once more, moving on him as he'd seen them move over a canvas. She had no idea what she was doing to him . . . nor what he could do to her. There she was, his beautiful guileless Jenny, imploring him for something he wanted to give her so badly, he hurt.

"Did she tell you it's dangerous to touch a man there?" Gently he set her hand aside, but there was to be no easy relief for him. She'd set needs in motion that couldn't easily be conquered.

"I want to be dangerous." Her jaw was set in stubborn lines as she challenged him. "I want a sweaty, tangled coupling, Daniel."

The words were foreign on her innocent lips. Gwendolyn again, no doubt. Good Lord, he didn't know whether to thank the woman or to shoot her.

He cupped Jenny's face and tipped it toward his. "Jenny, I want you more than any man has ever wanted a woman, but I was waiting because I wanted you to have everything in its proper order . . . a courtship, an engagement, a wedding."

"I don't want to wait. This is not a . . . a whim, Daniel. It's a need. I need you here . . . and here." She placed her spread hands over her breasts, then on her abdomen. Moonlight streamed through the window, illuminating her lush body.

Daniel felt as if all the treasure in the world had been laid at his feet. Jenny was freely offering him what he wanted to take. Still, he hesitated.

Nobility. Honor. Protectiveness. Scruples. For weeks he'd told himself that was why he couldn't make love to her. There was only one reason left, and that was fear.

With the insight that sometimes comes in the

darkness when the day's worries are cast aside and the spirit is free, he realized that he'd postponed a physical union with Jenny because he was afraid. He'd failed too many people. He was terrified of failing Jenny, of not being wise enough and tender enough and strong enough to make the physical side of love special for a very special woman.

She was waiting for his answer, standing before him with the innate dignity that had captured his imagination from the moment he'd seen her.

"Daniel, teach me . . . please . . ."

He put a finger over her lips. He didn't want Jenny to beg. Not his Jenny.

"I want to take you to my bed and love you in a way that will banish all your doubts. I want to kiss every inch of your exquisite body and explore all your sweet, secret places. I want to love you, Jenny . . . not as your teacher, but as an equal."

Then his beautiful, artless Jenny stepped back and slid her gown from her shoulders. It cascaded to the floor in a silken heap, and she stood, revealed.

"See?" she said, lifting her breasts. "You do this to me."

"I want to do more, Jenny." He covered her breasts with his hands, reveling in their ripe weight and satiny texture. Her nipples responded instantly to his touch. "Tell me if you want me to stop . . . anytime, Jenny. Just say the word and I'll stop."

"Don't stop." Her face was filled with rapture. "Oh, Daniel. I like it. Please, don't stop."

He bent down and circled her nipples with his tongue. She caught his hair and instinctively pulled him closer.

Remarkable sensations were spilling through her body, feelings she'd never known existed. And all of them originated in her breasts, where Daniel lavished his attention.

She knew nothing except what Daniel had already taught her—that to kiss him was rapture, that to have him touch her skin set off Fourth of July sparklers along her nerve endings, that sometimes merely looking into his dark eyes made her feel buttery soft inside.

His hands were moving now, moving along her upper arms and down to the tips of her fingers. With his fingers lacing hers, he sucked her breasts.

She felt a moist heat blooming between her legs, and a restless driving need to get as close to him as possible. Cries like a small animal in pain escaped her throat, and she pushed her hips against him.

"Jenny . . ." His eyes were wide with concern as he looked down at her. "I don't want to scare you."

He bent down and scooped her gown off the floor. She would die if he stopped now.

"No." She put her hand out to stop him. "I don't understand this... sweet aching." She pressed her hands over her breasts. "I don't want it to stop."

"It won't stop, Jenny. It just gets better."

Daniel was so virile, so worldly. He'd done this hundreds of times with women far more sophisticated than she. Suddenly Jenny felt shy and uncertain. She folded her arms over her breasts and looked at him from under her lashes.

He brushed her hair back from her face, then gently removed her hands.

"Don't hide yourself from me, darling. You're very beautiful."

"You like seeing me naked?"

"Yes. I like it." He ran his hand from the base of her throat all the way down to her navel. Goose bumps rose on her skin. "You have an exquisite body. I want to touch you all over." His hands made small erotic circles on her abdomen. "May I, Jenny?"

"Please, Daniel... do."

He scooped her up and carried her to the bed. Daniel's bed. Oh, the joy of it. She spread her arms wide, feeling the cool sheets against her skin.

"The bed is cool and you're hot," she said.

His chuckle was low and sexy. "I certainly am, love. And you made me that way."

"I did?"

"Yes, you did. A woman who loves a man unconditionally as you do wields a great power over him."

"I don't want to wield power, Daniel. I want . . ." She didn't have the words to describe what she wanted. She lifted her eyes to his, hoping he'd understand.

It was all Daniel could do to keep from giving her everything she wanted in one blinding rush. He wanted to be inside her, feeling her hot flesh surround him. He wanted to hear the cries of pleasure in her throat and see the joy of discovery in her eyes.

With great effort he reined in his feelings. Jenny's were the ones that counted tonight.

"Let me show you what you want." He brushed her erect nipples with his fingertips, then traced a hot, sweet line downward. She was moist and swollen, and his fingers entered her slowly, delving briefly, then easing back.

"Daniel! It's . . . oh, it's better than flying."

Gwendolyn hadn't told her everything. She'd never imagined pleasure such as this. And with hands. Would hers do the same thing for him?

"If I touched you like that, would you like it, Daniel?"

"I would die from pleasure, my sweet Jenny."

"I don't want you to die. Not yet anyhow."

Her sassy reply delighted him.

His fingers parted her slick flesh, setting up a gentle rhythm. Jenny's breath quickened. He watched her face as he brought her closer and closer to the edge. She arched her back and pressed upward, then she splayed her hands out and clutched the sheets.

"Daniel . . . oh, Daniel."

"Go with the flow, sweetheart. Fly."

Jenny felt as if invisible strings were tugging at her whole body. She stiffened, trembling, then a hot, sweet explosion ripped through her, and she called Daniel's name.

He caught her close and pressed his face into her neck. "Sweet Jenny, sweet Jenny."

"I can't find the words, Daniel. 'Wonderful' is too pale for what I feel."

He lifted himself on his elbows and pushed her hair back from her face.

"Do you trust me, Jenny?"

"With my whole heart, Daniel."

"There will be a little bit of pain the first time."

"There's more?"

"Much more . . . but only if you want it."

She cupped his face and pulled it close to hers. "Show me, Daniel."

He kissed her on the tip of the nose, then slipped into the bathroom and readied himself for her.

She felt the great power of him as he levered himself over her. Already sensitized, her nipples came erect the minute his chest hair brushed against them. Sensations rippled through her as his heavy rigid flesh sought, probed, then slid into her. The flash of pain caught her unexpectedly. Reaching backward she caught the headboard.

"I'm sorry, sweet Jenny."

"No . . . it's all right." Impaled and not knowing what to do about it, she hung on to the headboard.

"There will be no more pain." She shook her head, afraid to open her mouth lest she cry out and make a fool of herself. "The rest is better . . . I promise."

Daniel began to move, sliding deeper and deeper. At first Jenny resisted, and then the most miraculous thing happened. The pain vanished and in its place was a wondrous pleasure such as she'd never known. Her heart, her whole body, sang for joy.

She wrapped her arms and legs around Daniel, wanting to hold him so close, he drowned in her. Her hips danced against his, and she whispered his name, over and over.

In this miraculous joining, it didn't matter that she was special. Her body knew what to do, and it was neither clumsy nor uncertain. She thought she would burst with joy.

And finally she did. Everything was hot and bright at the same time, and she fell, melting, against the sheets. Daniel rolled them to their sides, still joined, and lay stroking her face and hair.

"You're wonderful, Jenny. Magnificent."

She smiled a secret smile because she knew he spoke the truth.

"So are you," she said, feeling wise and generous and born anew.

NINE

They stayed in Raleigh three more days, giddy as teenagers and greedy as children. And when they came home at last, Daniel lingered on her doorstep, reluctant to let her go.

"You're my world, Jenny."

"And you're mine." She held on to both his hands, her eyes wide and earnest. "Can we be together the way we were in Raleigh?"

"Just let somebody try to stop us, Jenny. I'll turn them into dog food and sell them at Sullivan Stores."

He left her laughing on the doorstep. Jenny's beautiful image was still with him when he passed through his security gates and turned into his driveway, then it vanished as if it had been wiped out with black magic.

The car in front of Daniel's house made his

blood run cold. A red Fiat. Georgia license plates. Claire's car.

How the hell did she get through his security?

He gunned his car up the driveway, fishtailing as he rounded the oak tree. He was close enough to see her sitting in the driver's seat, black hair drawn back in a French twist that left curls curving onto her olive skin, full lips and dark eyes accented enough to enhance but not enough to detract. Everything about her was meant to look casual. Daniel knew from experience that appearances lied.

His tires squealed as he braked, and he was out of the car almost before it stopped. Rage propelled him across the driveway.

Claire let down her window. "Hello, Daniel," she said as calmly as if it had been only three days instead of three years since she'd seen him.

"Leave, Claire."

"Why, Daniel . . . is that any way to greet a wife?"

"You're no longer my wife."

"Is that why your hands are shaking?" He rammed his hands into his pockets. Her laughter was soft, intimate. "Is that why a muscle is twitching in your jaw and why your back is rigid? Because I'm no longer yours to do with as you please?" Her smoky voice dropped another octave. "And you were pleased quite often, weren't you, Daniel?"

"Damn you to everlasting hell."

They were locked together by the look that passed between them, locked together as surely as gladiators fighting to the death.

The sweet summer air trembled around them, full of cricket song and twilight. Beside the door, gardenia bushes perfumed the air. Recent rain had dampened the earth, and its rich fecund aroma surrounded them.

Everything around Daniel was filled with promise. And Claire had come to destroy it all.

Her bravado vanished as suddenly as it had come.

"You don't have to damn me to hell, Daniel. I'm already there."

She looked genuinely remorseful. Daniel hardened himself against her act.

"I don't know what impulse brought you here or what you hope to achieve by coming, but my advice to you is to leave before I have you removed for trespassing. You gave up all claims to me and the children three years ago."

"I can't leave, Daniel."

"Why? Is something wrong with your car?" He could be a tough, coldhearted bastard when the situation merited it . . . just like his father. A chilling thought.

"No, Daniel. Nothing's wrong with my car. I just came to talk."

"We have nothing to talk about."

"I think we do, Daniel." Claire fidgeted with the clasp on her purse, then looked him squarely in the eye. "I've come to get my children."

TEN

"I'll see you in hell first." Daniel jerked open the car door and started in. "Move over."

"Are you crazy?" Claire tried for defiance even as she scrambled out of his way.

Daniel got behind the wheel and roared out of the driveway. The tires screamed in protest as he took the curves.

"What are you doing?" Claire clutched the dashboard. Jaw clenched, Daniel ignored her. "You're going to get us both killed."

Daniel didn't stop until he got to a motel on the outskirts of town; then he jerked open the car door, marched Claire into the office, booked her for one night, and ordered a cab.

She was panting when he locked the bedroom door behind them.

"Now talk," he said. "You have fifteen minutes."

"Daniel . . . you've gone mad." Her hands shook as she reached into her purse for a cigarette.

"Fourteen."

With the lazy grace of a cat, Claire strolled to the bed and stretched out. Putting her hand on the mattress, she tested the springs.

"Ummm. Comfy. You always did know how to pick a bed, Daniel."

He glanced at his watch. "Thirteen."

"You're serious, aren't you?"

"Claire, I've always been serious. Life is not the game you seem to think it is."

"All right . . . all right." Her hands shook as she crushed her cigarette in the ashtray on the bedside table. "This is not a game. I want to see my children."

"By all the saints, why?"

"Because I love them."

He thought he'd see the lie in her face; instead he saw something that looked like emotion and a vulnerability he'd never expected.

"It's been three years, Claire. They barely remember you. I can't let you slip in and out of their lives on whim."

Claire paced the room, her lovely legs showing through the slit in her skirt. Every now and then she gave him a smoldering glance from underneath her long eyelashes. Daniel almost laughed. Why had he ever thought her beautiful and innocent?

"You can't or you won't, Daniel?"

"I won't. The children went through hell when you left the first time. I won't let you put them through hell again."

"I don't think you're going to have any choice in the matter." Claire swept her purse off the bed and made a great show of opening the clasp. She'd always been partial to the dramatic gesture.

When she threw the newspaper clipping onto the table, Daniel's heart stopped. A picture of two people kissing topped a lengthy article. He didn't have to look to know who they were.

"It's because of her, isn't it, Daniel?"

"Leave Jenny out of this, Claire. She has nothing to do with my decision."

"Well, she has something to do with mine." Claire jerked the clipping off the table and held it under his face. " 'Jenny Love-Townsend was seen smooching the elusive entrepreneur Daniel Sullivan at the grand opening of another Sullivan Store,' " she said, quoting from the article. " 'The famous Down's syndrome artist was wearing a ring said to be a Sullivan family heirloom.' "

Claire flung the paper across the room. "Do you think I'm going to leave my children in the hands of a *retard?*"

A Prince for Jenny

Daniel had never wanted to strike a woman until that moment. A muscle in his jaw ticked as he faced the woman who had once been his wife.

"I knew you had no morals, Claire. I never knew you were vicious."

"Morals! You preach to me about morals. I'll bet that little number can't wait to get her hands on your money . . . or is it your family jewels that interest her most?"

Only a massive effort at self-control kept him from giving vent to his rage.

"Your time is up, Claire." He started to the door.

"Do you think you can win that easily, Daniel? Do you think I'll slink off into the night after you walk out on me?"

"I don't give a damn what you do, Claire."

"You will, Daniel. You will."

Two things were paramount in Daniel's mind: checking on his children and checking on Jenny. He found his children in their bed already fast asleep. Miss Williams hovered anxiously in the hallway while he stood watch over each small bed.

Megan stirred, opened her eyes, then reached for him. "Daddy? I was dreaming you didn't come back."

"I'll always come back. Always." He kissed her sleep-warmed cheek, then tucked the covers under her chin. "Go back to sleep, sweetheart."

Patrick was curled into a tight ball with his fist under his cheek. A heavy sleeper, nothing could awaken him.

Daniel picked the teddy bear up off the floor and tucked it back into Patrick's arms. "Sleep fast, my son," he whispered. "I won't let any harm come to you."

Miss Williams was still waiting in the hallway when he came out. "Mr. Sullivan, is anything wrong?"

"Yes. Follow me, please."

In his study he gave his instructions. She was not to let the children out of her sight. She was never to entrust them to anyone whom Daniel had not specifically assigned to take care of them. He would give her a list of people who could talk to his children on the telephone; all other callers had to be approved by him.

"Tomorrow I'll enhance the security by hiring bodyguards who will accompany you and the children at all times. Do you have any questions or any problems with these changes?"

"Are the children in danger, Mr. Sullivan?"

Were they? Claire had been capable of leaving them without a word. Was she capable of taking them the same way?

A Prince for Jenny

"I honestly don't know, Miss Williams, but I have reasons to want extreme care taken with them."

"And my salary?"

"It will be handsomely increased."

"You can count on me, Mr. Sullivan." She lifted herself up to her full height. "Godzilla can't get past me when I make up my mind."

After the nanny left, Daniel sat at his desk pondering Claire's threat.

"I don't give a damn what you do, Claire."

"You will, Daniel. You will."

She'd been enraged about Jenny. Was there a chance Claire would try to harm her? It was a chance Daniel wasn't willing to take.

He posted one of his security guards outside the nursery, then drove to Jenny's. A light rain had begun to fall. His first instinct was to protect her without causing alarm. *Jenny's bright*, her doctor had said. *She understands everything*. He'd learned that lesson well in Raleigh. Not only did Jenny understand, but she wanted to be treated as if she did.

The rain picked up momentum, and he turned on his windshield wipers. In the closeness of the car, he got hot thinking of other things he'd learned in Raleigh.

Jenny was in the den playing a game of checkers with Gwendolyn. Her dogs were asleep at her feet, and the cats were curled on the sofa cushions. She took one look at Daniel's face and knew something was wrong.

Without a word she wrapped her arms around him and laid her head on his chest. His heart was pounding so hard, she could feel the vibrations in her cheek.

Taking his hand, she led him to the sofa. "Do you want tea first, or do you want to tell me what's wrong?"

Daniel smiled. "Are you clairvoyant, Jenny?"

"I talk with the angels."

Gwendolyn stood up and made a big to-do of yawning. "And it's time for me to talk to my pillow." Instead of bustling out the way she always did, she paused long enough to pat Daniel's cheek. "I always said you were the one to make Jenny's dreams come true."

He bent down and kissed her wrinkled cheek. Then, knowing how she hated to be thought sentimental, he frowned at her. "You wouldn't be trying for another gift, would you?"

"Poppycock. If I want a gift, I'll go out and find my own man." She'd dyed her hair red recently, and her bright curls bobbed as she headed up the stairs.

Jenny locked the door behind her, then put her arms around Daniel's neck.

"A kiss makes everything better, Daniel."

His mouth descended on hers. The tension of confronting Claire suddenly exploded, and he pulled Jenny hard against his hips, parting her legs with one of his. He could feel the softness and the heat of her through their clothes, and he went wild with need.

His tongue plied her mouth, thrusting hard and delving deeply. She moaned.

"Jenny?" He stepped back, apologetic. "I'm sorry. I went a little crazy."

Reckless fool. He'd been gentle with her in Raleigh, and patient. She was barely tutored in the ways of love. What was he trying to do? Scare her to death?

"No . . . Daniel . . ." She wrapped herself around him, her arms tight around his chest and her right leg hooked around his left. "Don't treat me differently."

By all the saints, would he never learn that lesson?

"I need you, Jenny."

"I'm here."

Even in his overpowering need, he didn't fail to prepare himself. Responsibility would always be a part of their lovemaking. It was a trust he'd taken on when he pledged his love to a special woman.

He gathered her skirt into one hand and hauled her close to him. The nearness of her made his heart slam against his chest. With their faces only inches apart, she looked deeply into his eyes.

"Don't be gentle with me, Daniel."

Never taking his eyes from hers, he lifted her up and wrapped her legs around his hips. His first thrust was hard and deep. Jenny's eyes widened.

"I like that . . . oh, Daniel, I like that a lot."

"You're going to like this even more." He began a frantic rhythm that sent them reeling against the walls. Sheer rapture colored Jenny's cheeks.

"Wonderful . . . wonderful . . . wonderful," she murmured as she rode the waves of sensation. If she'd known about such things, she might have compared their lovemaking to riding river rapids and racing down snowy ski slopes and plunging from great cliffs into the shining waters below. But all she knew was the wild freedom that filled her soul. She was soaring, soaring above all her handicaps, flying high above her limitations, flying with Daniel, her love, her hero.

There was something magnificent about his insatiable need. His eyes were bright as a god's as he took her to the floor. She met every thrust with joy, every new challenge with abandon.

He rolled them over. "Ride me, Jenny."

She needed no further instruction, for she was perfectly attuned to him, heart and soul and body. With her palms pressed against his and their fingers intertwined, she tried to fall into Daniel, to melt into him, to become a part of his hard, heaving body.

Lights from the lamp reflected on his dark hair, and brightness from the lightning that streaked the stormy skies shone in his hot eyes.

"Ah, Jenny . . . Jenny . . . Jenny."

Daniel's litany of praise was music to her ears. Some part of her that had long been held prisoner was released. She knew no boundaries as she loved her Daniel, no restraint. With hands and lips and eyes and body, she loved him, loved him until the sweat dripped into her eyes and she could hardly see, loved him until her dress became so tangled, she ripped it aside, loved him until at last they lay in a heap, hips still joined, arms spread at impossible angles, and legs heavy with the weight of each other and the weight of fulfillment.

Afterward they sat on the sofa, holding each other and sharing tender touches.

"You rescued me, Jenny."

"And you rescued me."

"I wish it could always be like this."

"It will."

Daniel almost believed her. But the ugly truth was, he knew things that she didn't know.

"Claire's back. She wants the children." He pressed his face into her hair. How could he tell her all Claire's ugly accusations without destroying her? "I'm afraid for them, Jenny. Afraid for you."

"Why?"

"She made threats. I don't know what she's going to do."

"I'll be brave."

"I know you will." He cupped her chin and turned her face to his. "I'm going to hire a bodyguard for you and a security guard for your house."

"No."

"Jenny, don't fight me on this. I can't risk something happening to you."

"I'm not fighting you, Daniel. But I'm fighting for myself. All my life somebody has watched over me. I want to make my own decision about this."

He knew she was right. If he wanted Jenny to emerge from her cocoon of overprotectiveness, he had to let her emerge all the way.

"I'll be careful, Daniel. I promise you. A mother has to stay safe for the sake of her children."

He rested his forehead against hers. "Jenny, do you know how much I love you?"

"I know, Daniel... but I wouldn't mind if you showed me again."

He laughed. "In a little while, Jenny. A man has to recover, you know."

"I'm learning."

Six days later Claire's lawyer filed a motion in the courts of Florence, Alabama, to bring forward and modify custody and visitation. She wanted her children back.

Daniel would have been relieved that she'd chosen legal means to fight him if he hadn't been so worried. There was no way in heaven or in hell he could keep Jenny from being involved in the custody suit.

"If she's going to be their stepmother, she's pivotal to this case, Daniel." His attorney fixed Daniel with a hard stare. "The best interests of the children will be the judge's only concern. He can't make that decision without questioning Jenny."

Fear squeezed Daniel's heart, fear for Jenny and fear for his children.

"Is there any way we can keep Jenny out of this?"

"Yes...only one." Lawrence Blakestone didn't have to elaborate. Daniel knew what that one way was: give up Jenny.

"No," he said, shaking his head. "Never."

"Are you sure you know what you're doing, marrying this woman?"

"I'm sure."

Heartsick, he left the attorney's office. In claiming Jenny, would he lose his children?

ELEVEN

Daniel couldn't keep the custody suit a secret from his children. According to law, their best interest could only be served by a guardian ad litem, their own lawyer. Her name was Margaret Case, a motherly woman who was a cuddly teddy bear with the children and a tiger in the courtroom.

She didn't try to hide her presence when she came to visit their home, but instead made herself a part of the family.

"This is wonderful soup," she said. Daniel sat at the head of the long table with Jenny on his right and the children on his left. Margaret sat beside Jenny so she could see the faces of the children.

"I made it," Megan said.

"All by yourself?" Margaret didn't approve of child labor.

"Course not. I'm just a little kid. But Jenny lets me help when she cooks."

"Do you like to cook, Megan?"

"Sometimes. I like games better."

"What kind of games?"

"Football and soccer and hopscotch." Megan was proud of her athletic abilities.

"Jenny fell playing hopscotch," Patrick volunteered. "Show your skint knee, Jenny."

"Maybe later." Although Jenny had told Daniel she would be brave, she knew she wasn't. She twisted her napkin into a wad, and it lay in her lap like a lump of coal. Daniel was smiling, but his smile didn't touch his eyes.

What if she was making a terrible mess of things? What if he lost his children because of her?

"Jenny's a great artist, you know," Daniel told Miss Case, "but she's never too busy to leave her work and play with the children. They love it."

"We love it," they said in unison, as if they'd been coached.

Jenny's spirits fell. She and Daniel and the children were wonderful together. What was happening simply wasn't fair.

"She did the portrait of the children that's hanging over the mantel." Daniel was too anxious on her behalf. Even Jenny saw that.

"It's beautiful," Miss Case said. Jenny could

tell from the tone of her voice that she was not interested in art.

"Thank you." Jenny knew she sounded like a simpleton. When she was nervous, she always had a harder time making her words come out right.

Helplessly she looked at Daniel. He smiled, trying to tell her everything was all right, but she knew better.

Things might never be all right again.

After he drove her home, they slipped upstairs to Jenny's bed.

"Let's get married now," he said.

"No."

"We can put together a fancy wedding in a few days."

"It's not the fancy wedding..."

She didn't have to say anything else. Daniel knew.

He pushed her gown from her shoulders, levered himself over her, and slid home. There was love in the way he moved inside her, and so much tenderness that she wanted to cry.

But not yet. Daniel might not understand.

She'd save the tears for after he was gone. For now, she would dance to this ancient music and smile, smile, smile.

Daniel had grown accustomed to the disruption of his life. Margaret Case didn't give warnings; she merely appeared, hoping to catch them in an unguarded moment, he supposed.

His muscles bunched along his neck and back as he stood at the mantel watching her observe Jenny and the children. He needed a massage. He needed peace. He needed Jenny.

The children had begun to relax around their audience, but Jenny hadn't. With each successive visit she became more and more tense. Her limp worsened, and sometimes she tripped over words she'd always found perfectly easy to say.

"Bedtime, children," Daniel said, glad the ordeal was almost over.

"We want a bedtime story," Patrick said.

"Of course." He went to the bookcase and pulled out two of their favorites, the Christopher Robin stories of A. A. Milne and Barrie's *Peter Pan*. "What would you like to hear?"

"This one." Megan plucked the A. A. Milne from his hands and handed it to Jenny. "Will you read it to us, Jenny?"

"Yeah, Jenny!" Patrick crawled into her lap, and Megan leaned on her knees.

The look Jenny cast him broke his heart. She was the best mother his children could possibly have, loving, sensitive, patient, kind. And yet she was made to feel unworthy . . . all because of Claire.

"Why don't we give Jenny a break, children?" he said. "She's been painting portraits all day."

" 'Cause she does Kanga better than you, Daddy. Piglet too." When Megan got that stubborn look on her face, it was dangerous to cross her. Besides, Daniel didn't want to make an issue with Margaret Case looking on.

"Which story do you want?" Jenny asked as she took the book.

"The one about the Woozle," Megan said.

It seemed to take forever for Jenny to find the right story. The silence in the room was deafening. Daniel wanted to take Margaret Case by the collar and escort her to the door, then he wanted to bundle up Jenny and his children and take them to Switzerland.

"Here it is." Jenny's obvious relief almost brought tears to Daniel's eyes. "Ready, children?" She touched their hair and smiled into their upturned faces. Only a fool would believe that she wouldn't make a good mother.

Daniel prayed that Margaret Case was no fool.

When Jenny started to read, he held his breath. With her fingers moving across the page, she read with excruciating slowness, halting frequently over words that any child would know.

Once, Megan leaned close to whisper the word Jenny stumbled over.

If he stopped the torture, Daniel would be damning Jenny as inadequate, and if he let it continue, he would be leaving her at the mercy of the woman sitting on the edge of her chair.

Jenny's hands trembled and her eyes were filled with despair.

Margaret Case be damned. Daniel couldn't stand by any longer. He'd started across the room when Jenny's chin came up. She closed the book, then took his children's hands.

"Would you like to hear the story in a new way?"

"Like what?" Megan, the little skeptic, asked.

"If you'll get my pad and pencil off the desk, I'll show you."

"I'll get it, I'll get it." Patrick raced off and was back in record time with the things she'd requested.

Jenny began to draw, and as she sketched the familiar figures of Winnie the Pooh and Christopher Robin and Piglet, her confidence returned. And with it the music of her lilting voice. She told the story as only Jenny could, in her guileless, straightforward way.

Megan and Patrick were spellbound.

"Look," Patrick shouted. "Jenny made a terrible Woozle."

"And the Wizzles too." Casting off her role as resident skeptic, Megan hopped up and down in her excitement. "Draw another one, Jenny."

"Yeah! Another one."

There was magic in the room. Daniel felt it; Margaret Case saw it. The three bent over the sketch pad had transcended the real world and entered into an enchanted place peopled with Wizzles and Woozles and filled with the happiness of childhood.

"Well, I guess I'll be going," Margaret Case said when the story ended. She didn't try to hide the tears in her eyes. Taking her handkerchief from her purse, she wiped her cheeks, then blew her nose. "My, I loved that story as much as the children did."

"I'll read one to you anytime."

There was no doubting Jenny's sincerity. Margaret took her hand.

"My dear, this has been a very special evening. In my line of work I rarely run across pure love and total innocence. I've seen them both here tonight."

After Margaret Case left and the children were upstairs in their beds, Jenny held Daniel's hands and danced around in her excitement.

"Daniel, we've won . . . we've won."

Bodyguards watched over the children as they slept, and somewhere in Atlanta, Claire was consulting with her attorney about the best way to prove Jenny's unfitness to be a mother.

They hadn't won yet, not by a long shot. But he couldn't bear to tell her so.

"You were wonderful, Jenny." He held her close. "Absolutely wonderful."

"And brave too." She smiled up at him. "You forgot brave."

"Yes. And brave too."

"Daniel, do you think I can start picking out a wedding dress now?"

"I want you to pick out the prettiest wedding dress in all of Florence."

"I used to dream about having a wedding of my own. . . . We're really going to be a family, aren't we, Daniel?"

"We'll be a family, Jenny. I promise."

He'd see Claire in hell before he broke his promise to Jenny.

Sarah never dreamed that she'd be shopping for a wedding gown for her firstborn. She and Gwendolyn sat in satin-covered chairs waiting for Jenny to come out of the fitting room.

Victoria emerged first, her unruly black hair slipping from its French twist and her green eyes sparkling.

"You ought to see my sister. It was worth the trip from Dallas." She'd left her law practice for the specific purpose of helping her half sister shop for the most important gown of her life.

"I can't wait," Gwendolyn said. "Come on out, honey. We want to see."

"Just a minute. I'm nervous."

"Lordy, what will she be on her wedding day?" Gwendolyn said.

Sarah and Victoria exchanged glances. They were both thinking the same thing. Would there be a wedding day for Jenny? Victoria knew the law. Although there was no presumption that Jenny would be an unfit mother, any lawyer worth his salt would use her condition to try to prove that she was not only unfit but also a danger to Daniel's children.

One big question loomed in the minds of Jenny's family: If Daniel lost his children, would he still marry Jenny?

The curtains to the dressing room parted, and out stepped Jenny. Tears sprang to Sarah's eyes, and Gwendolyn surreptitiously sniffed into her handkerchief. Only Victoria remained calm.

"You're beautiful, Jenny," she said. "You're going to take Daniel's breath away."

"You really think so?"

"Come out to the mirror so you can see for yourself."

Jenny could hardly believe that she was the woman in the mirror. The gown looked like something Cinderella might have worn to the ball. It transformed Jenny from a woman with vast limitations to a woman with endless possibilities. Wearing the gown, she looked as if she were going off to meet her prince.

"I want to show Daniel."

"Are you sure, Jenny?" Sarah asked. "The tradition is to keep the bridal gown a secret from the groom until the wedding day."

"People are more important than tradition." Daniel needed something beautiful in his life right now. Jenny caught Victoria's hand. "Will you help me get it off and into a box?"

Sarah and Gwendolyn cried openly after the sisters went back into the dressing room.

"Gwendolyn, what will we do if there is no wedding?"

"You hush talking like that." Gwendolyn adjusted her Panama hat. She wore it everywhere, even to church. "I thought you and Jake Townsend would never get together, and look how all that turned out."

With her heart-shaped lips and her blue eyes, Sarah looked almost as young as her firstborn.

Jake Townsend was her hero. Always had been and always would be.

"You're right, Gwendolyn." Sarah blew her nose on a pink tissue. "How silly of me to worry so."

Claude Sullivan hadn't expected a warm reception from his son, but he'd expected better than he was getting. Daniel's eyes were pure ice, and if faces could start wars, his would.

"There's no need for this animosity, Daniel. I'm merely offering advice."

"I didn't ask for your advice. If that's why you came all the way from Virginia, you wasted your time."

Daniel didn't even call him Father. Claude hadn't realized how that hurt until now. Maybe he was getting old, too old to try and make his wayward son see the truth.

"Okay. I admit I was wrong about your choice of career." Daniel's silence was more damning than words. "But I'm not wrong about this."

The source of all the trouble lay on Daniel's desk, a copy of the *Alexandria Beacon*. The now-famous photograph of Daniel and Jenny exchanging a kiss at the grand opening of his store in Raleigh stared up at them.

Daniel didn't even bother to read the article.

He could guess what it said. In spite of Jenny's remarkable accomplishments, the press chose to focus on only one thing—her limitations.

With swift movements Daniel tore the news article to shreds and dropped them into his wastebasket.

"I'll drive you back to your hotel," he said, standing up.

Defeat didn't sit well with Claude. Besides that, he'd lost Daniel years ago. Now he had nothing left to lose.

"I won't be dismissed like one of your hired hands." When Claude stood up, he was as tall as his son. They had the same square jaw and the same probing black eyes. Time had whitened Claude's hair and lined his face, but it hadn't moderated his temper nor cooled his determination. "I came to have my say, and I plan to say it."

"Have your say, but it will change nothing."

"How can you be so cavalier about something this important? By all the saints, Daniel, your future is at stake here." Claude jerked up the wastebasket and dumped it on Daniel's desk. Pawing through the torn bits of newspaper, he came up with a piece that showed Jenny's face. "Just look at her, son. Is she worth losing your children over? Do you think Jenny can give you children? Or has that ever crossed your mind?"

"You've said enough." Daniel was fighting hard for control.

"I haven't said nearly enough." Claude was shaking now, but he wasn't about to let that stop him. "She'll be an embarrassment to you, Daniel. She's already made you a laughingstock coast to coast."

"Leave!"

"No, not until I finish."

"You're already finished."

"If you marry her, you'll be no son of mine."

"I stopped being a son of yours the day Michael died."

The old pain rose up in Claude like a red cloud, obscuring everything except his rage.

"You chose a slut the first time around, Daniel. Did you do any better this time?"

Daniel hit him. Bone slammed against bone, and Claude felt the shock all the way to his toes. For a moment he thought he would go under, but he battled against it.

Silence screamed around them. Daniel's face was a hard, cold mask. Only his eyes were alive. They were bright with stubborn pride and anger and . . . Was that regret?

Claude waited, waited for an apology he knew would never come. Finally he left the office, not with his head bowed like a defeated old man, but with his back held rigid and his chin held high.

The door slammed shut behind him.

Daniel slumped into his chair and stared at the wreckage on his desk.

"What have I done?"

Jenny tried to make herself invisible. Crunched in a doorway watching Daniel's father leave, she wrapped her arms tightly around herself so she wouldn't shake. She'd die before she'd face him.

His footsteps echoed down the hallway. When she heard the elevator door close, she started running, running toward the stairs. She had no plan, no place to go. All she knew was that she had to leave.

She was still shaking when she got into her car. The car Daniel had given her. Daniel who would never have any more children because of her. Daniel who would be embarrassed because of her. Daniel who was the laughingstock of the country because of her.

The engine purred to life the instant she turned the key. Fighting the tears that blinded her, she drove through Florence and across the Tennessee River. Somewhere far behind her, Daniel would be sitting at his desk in Sullivan Enterprises.

Would he miss her when she was gone?

Daniel wasn't aware of time. All he knew was pain.

The sun was setting when he finally left his chair. Soon it would be time to go home, time to see his children, time to talk with Jenny.

Jenny.

His knuckles smarted. He held his hand up and studied it as if it didn't even belong to him. There was blood where he'd broken his skin. A little water would wash the blood away.

But what would wash away the guilt?

The hallway outside his office was quiet. Had everybody gone home?

As Daniel strode toward the water fountain he saw the box, a large white dressmaker's box. Fancy Fashions, the label proclaimed. It wasn't like Helen to leave things lying around. Where the devil was she?

Daniel picked up the box, and out spilled the gown. His heart slammed against his ribs. The dress was white satin encrusted with pearls. A wedding dress.

His hand trembled as he touched the cool satin. A bill slipped out of the folds of the gown and fluttered to the floor. The name at the top was Jenny Love-Townsend.

She'd been here. She'd heard it all.

"JEN-NYY!"

Helen rushed down the hall, her hand over her heart.

"Daniel?" He was standing with a wedding gown in his hand and his head bowed. "Mercy, you scared me to death."

"Was Jenny here?" Foolish question. He was holding her wedding gown.

"Yes. I thought she was with you." Helen took the dress from him and carefully arranged it in the box. "I can't imagine why she left her dress. She wanted to show it to you."

"What time did she come?" *Give me a miracle, God,* Daniel prayed.

"While your father was here."

Daniel died inside. In loving Jenny, he'd destroyed her.

"Did she say where she was going?"

"No. I didn't even see her leave. I told her she could wait in my office, but she said she'd go on down and surprise you. I thought you might like her to meet your father." Helen put her hand back over her heart. "I hope I didn't do anything wrong."

"No, Helen, you didn't do anything wrong."

He was the one who had done wrong. He'd dragged a total innocent into the mess that was his life and exposed her to public ridicule.

There was nothing he could do to make everything all right, nothing he could say to take back the hateful words that had been said against her. The only thing he could do was apologize and give her a chance to pull out of a very bad bargain.

But first he had to find her.

TWELVE

Daniel didn't know where to start looking. Would Jenny go home, or would she go to his house and wait for him? She might even go to her parents.

He drove to Jenny's first, looking for her car. It wasn't in the driveway. Every nerve ending in his body was screaming. Gripping his steering wheel, he stared at her empty driveway and tried not to panic.

Jenny could be anywhere. Shopping, perhaps. Or eating ice cream. Jenny loved ice cream.

Maybe she hadn't overheard the conversation in his office. Maybe she'd suddenly remembered an errand she had to do and had forgotten to take her wedding gown with her.

Fool. He'd known the truth the minute he saw the wedding gown.

Jenny's house mocked him. So safe. So serene.

So empty. Even her house was no longer a haven for her. He'd taken that away too.

He broke all the laws as he raced toward his house. One thought was in his mind—find Jenny.

Jenny sat under the oak tree, looking out over the river. It was the tree where she and Daniel had picnicked. She touched the tree's rough bark and its glossy leaves. She gazed upward remembering how the sun had looked filtering through the leaves. Someday she would paint the tree, paint it exactly as it had looked the day she'd received her first kiss.

Jenny touched her lips. Daniel would never kiss her again, never touch her, never make love to her. There would be no more picnics, no more more movies, no more laughter.

She put her hand over her heart to stop the hurting. The sun vanished and darkness crept over the land. She was silly to be sitting under a tree in the dark. She might not even be safe.

Hurrying, she got behind the wheel of her car. She didn't have a plan; all she knew was that she had to get away. When she got where she was going, she'd write letters to everybody. Maybe Gwendolyn would come and join her. They'd set up another studio far away from Daniel.

Someday he'd forget her. But she would never forget him. Never.

Daniel had looked in all the places she might be: his house, her parents' house, the ice cream parlor, the park. He'd even gone to the river where they had had their first picnic.

Fighting against his rising fear and the sense of defeat that threatened to swamp him, Daniel paused to formulate a plan. There was no need to alarm anyone, not yet. She couldn't have gone far. First he'd comb every square inch of Florence. If her car was still in town, he'd find it.

On the outskirts of Florence, Jenny came to her senses. After all her brave talk to Daniel, here she was running away like a scared rabbit. Oh, she was selfish to the core, thinking only of herself. The words she'd overheard had hurt her. But what about Daniel? Had she even considered how he must feel?

And what about the children?

Jenny pulled into a fast-food place and sank into a corner booth.

"Take your order, hon?"

She wasn't hungry, but she didn't want to

hurt the woman's feelings. "A hamburger, no onion."

The waitress slipped away on her spindly shoes, chewing her gum and humming.

Jenny remembered when she'd hummed. Daniel made her hum... and his children, and all their animals. Goodness gracious, she was so selfish, she'd left her animals behind.

"A pretty pickle you're in, Jenny Love-Townsend."

"What's that, hon?" The waitress slid the hamburger onto the Formica tabletop.

"I was just talking to myself."

"We all do it sometimes." Lou Eva, her name tag said. "If it'll help any, you can talk to me."

"I don't want to take up your time."

"Nothing much goin' on around here." Lou Eva slid into the opposite side of the booth, then wrapped her gum in a paper napkin. Southern from the tips of her painted red fingernails to the soles of her spike-heeled shoes, she loved nothing more than a good thorny problem—as long as it belonged to somebody else. "This town is dead as a doornail. I'm thinking about going to Birmingham myself. I hear they got some action down there."

"I'm leaving town too."

"You don't look too happy about it, hon."

"I'm not."

"Then don't go."

How simple that sounded. *Don't go.*

"Listen, hon." Lou Eva leaned across the table and took Jenny's hand. "We women gotta stick together. You just tell old Lou Eva what's botherin' you, and I'll try to help you out. I been around the track a time or two. There ain't nothin' I haven't seen and nothin' I can't fix."

Jenny knew she was seeing true courage. For all her bragging to Daniel about being brave, she'd turned and run at the first sign of trouble. She was a coward and a deserter . . . no better than Claire. And like Claire, she was abandoning Megan and Patrick.

How would that look to a judge? It was something that had never crossed her mind. She'd also never considered the fact that she barely knew her way around Florence, let alone the rest of the state. What judge was going to put Megan and Patrick in the hands of a woman who flitted off at the first sign of trouble and didn't even bother to take a map?

If she wanted a judge to call her fit, she had to act fit.

"You know what?" She leaned toward her new friend. "I think I can fix things, too, Loeva."

"Lou Eva, hon. But don't fret about it. I been called worse."

"Sometimes I don't get things right the first

time. But I get them right the second." Jenny stood up and hugged the waitress. "Thanks, Lou Eva."

"All in a day's work, hon." She lightly punched Jenny's arm. "Go get 'em, tiger."

When Jenny left the fast-food place, she had a plan. Confront the enemy. It didn't take her long to find him, for Florence wasn't blessed with places to stay and Helen had told her his name.

She called him from the lobby of his hotel.

"This is Jenny Love-Townsend."

There was a dreadful silence at the other end of the line. Jenny squeezed her eyes shut, hoping as hard as she could that he wouldn't say no.

"I have nothing to say to you, young woman."

"I don't mean to be pushy, but I'd love to meet you."

"I'll give you five minutes. That's all."

Claude Sullivan looked so much like Daniel, she could have picked him out in a crowd. But he had none of Daniel's warmth, none of his charm, none of his humor.

He didn't offer her a chair, nor did he apologize for making her meet him in his room. She stood beside the door, trying to look more confident than she felt.

"Mr. Sullivan . . . I'm Jenny."

"I know who you are. You're just like your picture. Beautiful women have always been Daniel's downfall."

"Daniel values character more than beauty."

"Bosh!"

They were not off to a good start. Jenny found herself casting about for the right words to say what she wanted.

"Well . . . I thought you came to talk." Claude Sullivan stalked to a chair. He didn't move like an old man, but he sat down like one, loose-jointed and heavy. "Talk." He glared at her from under his heavy brows.

Jenny began to talk, not with eloquent words and dramatic gestures but from the heart. She told how she and Daniel had met, how he had worn a yellow rose in his lapel and how she had known he was her hero. She told about their jog and their dance in the moonlight and their picnic. She even told about their first kiss.

Daniel's father sat very still. Not one single movement or facial expression betrayed his thoughts. There was nothing Jenny could do except hope.

"He didn't see me as other people do, Mr.

Sullivan. He saw me with his heart, and I saw him with mine."

Claude Sullivan was unmoved. Jenny trembled near the doorway, torn between flight and fight.

She made one last overture of peace.

"We are going to be a family, and I hope you will be a part of it." Guided by instinct, Jenny crossed to Daniel's father, knelt beside his chair, and took one of his hands. "I know I'm different, Mr. Sullivan. I don't talk well and I don't walk well. But I can love. I can love as well as anybody in the whole world. I love Daniel and the children, and I hope you will let me love you too."

Claude Sullivan sat in stony silence. There was absolutely no indication that he had even heard Jenny, let alone heeded her. She held his hand a while longer, then gently she laid it back in his lap.

The space between the chair and door seemed as vast as a scorching desert in Egypt. Leaning down, she kissed Daniel's father on the cheek, then she crossed that endless desert . . . alone.

After the door closed behind her, Claude continued sitting in his chair. It was getting dark, but he didn't bother to turn on the lights. He reached for the remote control and switched on the television. It didn't matter what was playing, as long as it made noise.

Groucho Marx and his brothers cavorted across the screen. Canned laughter echoed in the room. The glow from the television screen fell across Claude's face and illuminated his tears.

Daniel was near panic. He'd been driving for hours, and there was no sign of Jenny's car anywhere. Weary, he turned toward home.

It was getting late. The children would be ready for bed, and he wanted to be there to tuck them in. Then he'd have to call Jake Townsend. It would be one of the hardest phone calls he'd ever made.

Jenny was watching out the window for Daniel's car. When she saw the headlights, she waited for him at the front door.

She heard his key turning in the lock, and suddenly he was there, frozen in the doorway, holding her white satin wedding gown, a dozen emotions crossing his face. Jenny saw them all—relief, joy, pain, and then something she'd never expected, a sorrowful resignation.

Oh, Daniel, say something, her heart cried out.

He watched her, as still as his father had been. Only his eyes were alive.

The clock in the hallway chimed the hour,

and outside the cicadas sang their summer song. Miss Williams tiptoed down the stairs and into the kitchen to make herself a cup of tea. There was a muffled sound upstairs as the bodyguards positioned themselves for their night watch over Daniel's children.

Daniel's muscles bunched into tight knots, and he clenched his jaw so hard, he almost broke teeth. Every fiber in his body was crying out for Jenny. He wanted nothing more than to take her in his arms and pretend that nothing had happened.

But he could no longer be the instrument of Jenny's destruction.

"Jenny, I know what happened this afternoon. I'm so sorry." He laid the gown across the Queen Anne chair.

"It's all right."

"No. It's not all right." Nothing would ever be all right again. "Let's go into my study so we can talk."

Why didn't he touch her? Forlorn and uncertain, Jenny followed him into the book-lined room. Daniel closed the door.

"Can I get you anything, Jenny?"

How polite. Like a stranger.

"No, thank you." She sat in a deep leather chair. "Are you mad at me, Daniel?"

"Mad at you?" He knelt beside her chair and

pressed her hand, palm up, to his lips. His kiss was soft, oh so soft. Jenny closed her eyes. "I could never be mad at you."

His lips lingered on her hand. She was warmed by the nearness of him, warmed and comforted.

Abruptly he let go. Her eyes snapped open, and he walked quickly to the opposite side of his desk.

"I shouldn't have run away," she said.

"Anyone would have run away under those circumstances. What my father said about you was cruel and unconscionable."

"Fathers worry about their children."

"Jenny . . . Jenny . . ." Daniel began to pace the room. "You're too good . . . too kind . . . too generous."

He rammed his hands into his pockets, for that was the only way he could keep from touching her. When he reached the mantel, he saw the magnificent portrait she'd done of his children. Every line, every brush stroke, was filled with love. Gazing up at the portrait, Daniel remembered the day Jenny had started painting it. She'd been so innocent, so full of joy . . . so safe.

And now look at her. She was beleaguered on every side. And all because of him.

"Your gift never ceases to amaze me." He leaned against the mantel, facing her. "You're an extraordinarily talented artist, and no one can take that away."

Fear climbed in Jenny's chest, and she pressed her hand over her heart. Daniel was so remote that he might as well have been in another country.

"I had a lot of time to think while I was driving around Florence, Jenny. What I've done to you can't be undone, but it doesn't have to continue."

Daniel didn't want her anymore. She felt a terrible cry welling up in her throat, and she bit down on her lip to keep from making it. By running away, she'd destroyed everything. Daniel needed a woman, not an irresponsible child.

Slowly Jenny removed her engagement ring. Daniel's grandmother's ring. How she had loved it.

It stuck on her knuckle, and she had to twist hard to get it off. Daniel's eyes were terrible as he watched her. Why didn't he say something?

I love you, Daniel. I love you. Oh, she longed to say the words, but it would seem like begging. He was giving her a graceful way out. The best thing she could do was take it.

She held the ring tightly in her palm for a moment, memorizing its precious weight. Then she laid it on the table.

Daniel couldn't move. He felt as if a concrete slab were pressed against his chest. She was taking the opening he offered. Who could blame her? Love should be a beautiful dream, not the peril-filled nightmare he'd given her.

I love you, Jenny.

To say the words aloud would be cruel. He couldn't bind her to him with love words and love sighs, then continue to expose her to the thoughtless cruelty of his high-pressure world. He had to let her go.

His Jenny. His angel. His life.

Before she turned to go, she regarded him with her solemn blue eyes. He fell into their center, tumbled through the brightness until he was drowning in love.

Fingernails bit into flesh as he squeezed his hands into fists. To feel her lips upon his once more, to touch her satin skin, to feel her close around him in sweet, torturous clenches—that would be heaven.

His heaven and her hell.

"Good-bye, Daniel." Even her pronounced limp could not destroy her dignity and grace. At the door she turned. "Please tell the children I will always love them."

Oh, God. His children. How could he ever tell his children they'd lost Jenny?

"I will, Jenny."

In the doorway she hesitated. He couldn't bear to tell her good-bye.

Walk away, Jenny. Walk away. Quickly while I can still let you go.

The door closed softly behind her. He picked up the ring and held it in his fist.

"I love you, Jenny," he whispered. "I'll always love you."

He pressed the ring to his lips, then he sat in Jenny's chair and stared, dry-eyed, at the portrait.

Outside his study Jenny leaned her head against the door. "I will always love you, Daniel," she whispered.

Gathering her courage, Jenny walked away, past the kitchen where they'd baked cookies with the children, past the dining room where they'd shared so many happy meals.

She glanced up the winding staircase. Daniel's bedroom was up there somewhere. She'd never even had a chance to see it. Never had a chance to share his bed.

When she reached the hall and saw her wedding gown, she reached out and her hands sank into the cool satin folds. How happy her dreams had been . . . and how foolish. The gown slipped from her fingers, and she left it hanging carelessly across the chair. She wouldn't be needing it anymore.

The front door felt so heavy, she could barely push it open. Her entire body felt broken, shattered into a million tiny pieces.

Outside, a sudden summer storm caught Jenny by surprise. She stood on the front doorstep with the wind whipping her hair and the rain lashing her body. Driving home was going to be difficult. She'd have to be careful, that was all.

"Jenny!"

Daniel's voice slashed through her like a knife, and her heart lay bleeding in her chest. Slowly she turned back. The lights from the house poured over him as he ran toward her.

"Jenny, wait."

Had he come to tell her everything was all right? Had he come to give back her dream?

"You can't drive in this storm."

"I'll be careful."

He was beside her now. Gently he took her arm.

"Please, Jenny. Stay."

She wanted to stay more than anything in the world. She wanted to stay forever.

"I'll stay," she said. "At least until the storm is over."

Holding on to her elbow, he led her back inside. Neither of them looked at the wedding gown abandoned in the hallway.

"You're soaked," Daniel said as he escorted her back to his study.

"I'm just a little wet."

"You'll get sick."

"It's summer. The rain is warm."

"I'll get you some dry clothes."

"I don't want any."

They didn't look at each other when they talked. Neither of them could bear the pain. The study door clicked shut behind them, and at last Daniel turned toward Jenny. Her rain-soaked clothes clung to her body in delicious ways, and he almost reeled with desire. Clenching his jaw hard against the passion that rocked him, he poured her a brandy.

"Drink this." Her fingertips burned his where they touched. He hurried toward the door.

"Daniel... where are you going?"

"To get you some dry clothes."

Left alone in the study, she took a large drink of brandy. It sent little trails of fire shooting along her nerve endings, but it did absolutely nothing to dull her pain.

The house was quiet except for the rain beating against the windowpanes and the massive clock that ticked off the hours. Everybody would be in bed, dreaming their peaceful dreams.

Jenny remembered the brave words she'd said to Gwendolyn the day she'd met Daniel.

"Dreaming won't hurt," she whispered. Her voice echoed in the empty study.

She'd been wrong. She'd forgotten who she was and what she was. She'd been foolish and unrealistic, dreaming dreams that never had a chance of coming true.

But if she had it to do all over again, she'd do the same thing. Her memories were worth the pain.

The door opened, and Daniel came through carrying a large man's robe and man's shirt in his hands.

"I hope these will do."

"Thank you." The wonderful scent that was uniquely his clung to the fibers.

"While I was upstairs, I turned down the guest bed for you."

"I'm not staying."

"It's too late to drive home, even if the rain stops."

"I don't need you to take care of me." *Liar, liar, pants on fire.*

"I know you can take care of yourself. You were doing it very well before I came along."

She hated the way he looked, bone-tired and defeated.

"I'll stay, Daniel."

"I promise you, Jenny . . . no harm will come to you."

THIRTEEN

Daniel's guest bedroom looked as if it had never been used. Furnished with heavy antiques, it was austere and uninviting. Jenny lay in the big bed, hugging Daniel's shirt to her body. She would have taken down the heavy draperies and put a huge green plant by the window. If she'd married Daniel, she'd have put bright pillows on the bed and chairs, and simple oils on the wall.

She heard Daniel's footsteps in the hallway. He paused briefly outside her door, then hurried on.

I promise you, Jenny. No harm will come to you.

Oh, Daniel. She turned her face into the pillow. Their love had been so beautiful. How could it vanish in such a short time?

Somewhere down the hallway she heard a door open and shut. Daniel was in his bedroom now . . . alone.

Jenny tossed and turned, bunching his shirt under her in an uncomfortable wad. She sat up and turned on the bedside lamp.

She straightened the shirt, then snapped off the light and lay back down. Exhaustion caught up with her, and she dozed.

Rain beat a steady rhythm against her windows. Lightning streaked the sky and thunder rumbled. Jenny came awake suddenly, filled with a sense of urgency so overwhelming, she could barely breathe.

She put on Daniel's robe and went in search of him.

Daniel sat in the dark, staring in the direction of the portrait. The door to his study eased open, and he started from his chair.

"Daniel?"

Jenny was hardly more than a shadow in the doorway. Dwarfed by his robe, she glided toward him, her bare feet soundless on the hardwood floors.

"Jenny, what are you doing up?"

"I forgot something, Daniel. Something very important."

She was standing so close that he could reach out and touch her. Daniel prayed for strength to resist.

"What is it, Jenny?"

"I forgot to tell you that I love you." Silent screams ripped through him. "I'm not trying to win you back, Daniel. I know it's over. But I want you to know that I'll always love you."

The stillness in the room was complete. Above the folds of the dark robe, her face and eyes were luminous. Jenny. His angel in disguise.

Prickles danced along the back of his neck, and muscles bunched in tight cords along his shoulder blades. He held tightly to the arms of his chair, afraid he'd reach out to her if he weren't anchored.

Silently she turned to leave. His robe trailed behind her, swooshing softly on the polished floor.

"Jenny . . ."

She stopped, made a half turn. The rain had stopped, and the moon had broken through the clouds. His oversized clothes had slid from one shoulder, and a pale sliver of moonlight illuminated her dewy skin.

Daniel's hands tightened on the chair arms.

"I had to release you, Jenny, not because I don't love you, but because I love you too much."

"You still love me, Daniel?" Keeping her distance, she faced him.

"I never stopped loving you. But you've been hurt because of me. You've been insulted and ridiculed. I couldn't let that happen to you anymore."

"You didn't stop wanting me, Daniel?"

"Is that what you thought? That I didn't want you anymore?"

With her hands clasped tightly in front of her, she nodded.

Daniel's control broke. He bolted from his chair and folded Jenny in his arms.

"I'll never stop wanting you, Jenny. Never." They held on to each other, swaying. "This afternoon when I discovered you'd overheard the conversation in my office, I thought I might never see you again."

"I meant to leave Florence."

"What stopped you?"

"The thought of you and the children. I couldn't leave you, Daniel."

He'd been a fool to let her go.

"Don't ever leave me again, Jenny."

His lips descended on hers, and he kissed with the intensity of a soldier returning from war. He couldn't get enough of her. If he lived to be a hundred, he would never get enough of Jenny.

When they drew apart for breath, he led her

to the wing chair, then took her hand and knelt at her feet.

"Jenny, the last time around I didn't propose to you properly. I'm on my knees begging your forgiveness for being a blind fool." He kissed her hand. "Will you marry me, Jenny?"

"I will, Daniel."

"Will you wear my ring and never take it off?"

"I'll be proud to wear your ring."

He slipped it on her finger, then lifted her into his arms and sat back in the chair with her cuddled against his chest.

Jenny was back where she belonged, but she'd learned a very hard lesson. She was no longer in the protected environment created by Jake Townsend; she was in the real world, a world that dished out equal portions of bad and good, a world that could be as thoughtless and cruel as it could be beautiful and kind. Holding on to her dream was not going to be easy.

"I'm afraid, Daniel. Not for myself but for the children."

"Don't be afraid, Jenny. We're together now. No matter what happens, we'll find a way to make everything work." He pressed his cheek against her soft hair. "I promise you."

He carried her upstairs to his room and laid

her on his bed. With her bright hair spread over the pillow, she looked like a fallen flower. He undressed her slowly, stripping away the clothes that were too big and unveiling the perfection that was Jenny.

There was no need for words between them. She lifted her arms and he wrapped himself in her sweet embrace. Beneath his hard body she felt fragile, but he knew better. There was strength and power and fire in Jenny. And he wanted to claim it all.

She cupped her hands under her breasts and offered them up to him. His mouth closed over her rosy nipple, and she sighed.

Daniel was home where he belonged.

Claire had waited all summer to have her day in court. The hearing was finally set for September 15. She'd chosen her clothes carefully, and she knew she looked good—demure, understated, sincere. Her suit was wool crepe, navy blue with an innocent white blouse. She looked as sincere as sin.

Daniel was sitting across from her, handsomer than she remembered. If he'd been half as interested in her as she'd been in him, she'd never have left him. His fiancée was with him. Claire wondered what he saw in her. She was the quiet, mousy type. Beautiful, she'd grant that. Daniel always could pick a pretty woman. But why in the name of heaven would he want a retarded woman?

Not that Claire was complaining. It made her job easier. No judge in the country was going to let him keep custody of the children and put them in the hands of a woman who probably couldn't spell her own name.

Claire's name was being called. She took the stand. Her lawyer was good. They went over everything they'd rehearsed. Claire even cried on cue.

Her conscience didn't hurt her the least bit. She *did* want her children back. She'd missed them.

Daniel's lawyer wasn't so easy on her.

"Did you leave your children three years ago?"

"It wasn't like that. Daniel was never home and I—"

"Answer the question. Yes or no. Did you leave your children?"

"Yes."

"Where did you go?"

"In town. Atlanta."

"Specifically."

"To a motel."

"And was someone else there to meet you?"

A Prince for Jenny

"Well, Daniel was never there..."

"I don't want to know about Daniel. We know who he was with: the children. What I want to know is who you were with."

"Jimmy Gratz."

"Jimmy Gratz. You left your husband and your children to be with Jimmy Gratz."

"You make it sound like something awful. It wasn't... it was..." Claire covered her hands and burst into tears. Real ones this time. She dug around in her purse, pulled out a tissue, and wiped her eyes. It came back black. Her mascara was running, but she didn't care. She was going to lose her children for good.

"I'm not a bad mother; I just made a mistake. I love my children. I love them!"

Claire's performance moved Jenny to tears, but Daniel remained unconvinced. Why now? After three years of silence, why did she suddenly proclaim to love the children?

Jenny's name was being called. He squeezed her hand.

"Don't worry, Jenny. You'll do great."

"I'm not worried."

Jenny took the stand. The fate of his children rested with her.

Daniel's lawyer, Lawrence Blakestone, had said he would ask her only one question. Jenny knew what it was going to be, but she wasn't certain what she would say. She'd practiced with Gwendolyn over and over, but nothing had come out right. She'd ended up sounding like a simpleton and making herself nervous.

"Claire's lawyer will try to discredit you, Jenny," Mr. Blakestone had said. "Forgive me for being blunt, but he'll try to make you look as if you don't have enough sense to take care of two children. He'll even try to prove that you're a danger to them. But remember this, Jenny. The burden of proof is on them. You are not presumed to be unfit merely because you were born special. Your response to my question should dispel any doubts the judge might have."

Jenny folded her hands in her lap and forced herself to remain calm as she waited for Mr. Blakestone's question.

"Jenny, I want you to tell the court in your own words what kind of mother you will be to Daniel's two children."

Jake and Sarah slipped quietly into the back of the courtroom, and suddenly Jenny knew what she would say.

"When I was four years old, I didn't have a father, because mine ran away. But a wonderful man named Jake came into my mother's life and changed all that. He was there to pick me up when I fell down and to hug me when I cried. He sat by my bed all night when I had chicken pox and sang silly songs so I would forget about itching. He taught me to ride a tricycle and tried to teach me to play ball. I was too slow and too clumsy, but Jake loved me anyhow.

"He couldn't give me his bloodlines, but he gave me his heart.

"I will be the kind of parent to Megan and Patrick that Daddy has been to me. I will give them my heart."

Daniel could have shouted for joy. Jenny was magnificent. Nothing Claire's lawyer could say would counteract her eloquent pledge of love.

Daniel and Jenny stood in a cluster with Jake and Sarah outside the courtroom.

"You're wonderful, Jenny," Daniel said. "Simply wonderful."

"That's my girl," Jake said, smiling and hugging Jenny.

Jenny's mother beamed, adding her praise.

Sitting on a cold marble bench on the opposite side of the hallway, Claire couldn't help but feel envy. Once, Daniel had looked at her in the way he now gazed at Jenny. Once, she'd deserved those looks.

Sighing, she reached into her purse for a cigarette. Jenny wasn't half bad. As a matter of fact,

Claire felt a grudging admiration for her. If she lost, at least she'd have the satisfaction of knowing that her children were with a mother who loved them.

A flurry of activity at the north end of the courthouse caught her attention. The children's guardian ad litem was taking them to the judge's chambers. The matter could not be resolved in their best interests until Megan and Patrick were heard.

The cigarette dangled from Claire's hand as she strained her eyes for a glimpse of her children. As if invisible strings were pulling her, Megan turned. She lagged behind Margaret Case and stared openmouthed at Claire.

Claire half rose from her seat.

"Come along, Megan," Margaret Case said.

Megan stood on one foot and rubbed the back of her left toe against her right leg. Then she lifted a small hand and waved.

Her hands shaking, Claire sank back onto the bench.

Daniel hadn't missed a single moment of the exchange between his ex-wife and his daughter. He thought of the years of bitterness and estrangement with his own father; he thought of all the years and all the hurt.

Was he right to try to keep Claire away from the children?

Claire looked up and caught him staring.

"I really do love them, Daniel," she said softly.

He almost believed her. The cavernous hall echoed with silence.

"Why don't I get coffee for everybody while we wait?" he said.

For the first time since the hearing, Claire smiled at him.

Over the years, Judge Grace Norman had grown accustomed to these hearings, but she didn't like them. There was nothing to like about presiding over the division of a family in a court of law.

She smiled warmly at the two children sitting on the couch in her chambers. Patrick smiled back, but Megan gave her a look that said "I'm reserving judgment."

"Well, now . . . Would you like something to drink?"

"We're not thirsty." Megan spoke for both of them. She caught her brother's hand and gave Grace a proud, defiant look. Only the most discerning eye could see the slight tremble in her bottom lip.

Wishing for the wisdom of Solomon but settling for the wisdom of experience, Judge

Grace Norman began her task of determining the future of three adults and two children.

Later the judge looked at the solemn faces of the adults whose future rested with her.

"It is the opinion of this court that the children's best interests will not be served by removing them from the custody of their father."

Daniel Sullivan was not the emotional type. She'd known there would be no outbursts from him. But the look of joy on his face as he embraced his fiancée was one the judge would not soon forget.

"However, it is my belief that the natural mother is sufficiently penitent of her earlier actions and shows sufficient love for her children so that their interests will be served by allowing her generous visitation rights."

Claire Montague Sullivan's mascara was streaked to her chin, and she hadn't even bothered to wipe it away. Judge Norman thought that was a good sign.

"In the matter of Jenny Love-Townsend, I have this to say. If every child could have a mother like her, the world would be a better place."

FOURTEEN

The west wing of the Sullivan mansion was awash with silk petticoats and satin dresses, and in the bedlam, Gwendolyn reigned supreme.

She ushered Sarah to a chair and ordered her to stay there.

"I feel so foolish," Sarah said. "My own daughter's wedding, and I can't find my right hand with my left."

"I never saw a mother of the bride yet who wasn't a basket case." She gave Victoria the eye. "And that goes for sisters too."

"Who, me?" Victoria had her bridesmaid veil on backward.

"Yes, you." Gwendolyn sucked in her stomach and looked into the mirror.

"Lord, I look like a bale of cotton."

"Nonsense," Sarah said. "You're statuesque,

Gwendolyn, and with that hat you look like royalty."

"Daniel gave it to me." She arranged the frivolous concoction of tulle and lace on her curls. She'd let them go gray for the wedding. "He said he was scared I'd wear my Panama if he didn't get me a new one."

"I dreamed of many things for Jenny, but I never thought I'd see this day."

"That's because you couldn't know there was a Daniel Sullivan in the world. He's a very special man." Gwendolyn readjusted her hat. "And if anybody here says different, I'm going to black their eyes."

"What do you suppose is keeping Jenny?"

"Sit still, Sarah. I'll go see."

Jenny was sitting in a child's chair with Megan and Patrick on either side. On the small table in front of them was a sketch pad.

"Is that me?" Patrick asked, giggling.

"Yes," Jenny said. "That's you and this one is Megan."

"And you and Daddy," Megan said, pointing to two other figures.

"That's right. And after today we're going to be a real family."

"I'll put the names." Feeling important because she was the oldest and could spell,

Megan printed all their names underneath. When she'd finished, she puckered her brow. "What about mother?"

Jenny quickly sketched Claire. "She's part of the family too."

"She says you're nice," Patrick said.

"I think she's nice too. It's good to have two mothers who love you."

"And a brand-new grandpa and grandma and aunts and uncles." Megan beamed. "Put in Grandpa Jake, Jenny, and Grandma Sarah and Aunt Victoria and Uncle Josh and Uncle William."

Jenny added her parents and brothers and sister. The family was complete now—except for one. She walked to the window and searched the crowd for one face.

It was not there.

Megan tugged on her hand. "Jenny, tell us again how it's going to be."

"Yeah. Tell us." Patrick grabbed her other hand.

Jenny knew it was time to get dressed for her wedding, but she knew that children were more important than schedules. Daniel would wait.

She hugged them both. "You'll have two Christmases and two Easters and two vacations—one with your mother and one with us."

"On a bus?" Patrick said.

"Someday we'll go on a bus." Jenny drew

a recreational vehicle rollicking down the road, with children and animals hanging out the windows. In the driver's seat was Daniel, and riding shotgun was Jenny. Underneath she wrote *The Sullivan Family*.

Megan and Patrick pressed their little hands over the picture, then Megan counted the faces at the window.

"That's more than me and Patrick."

Jenny looked at all the tiny faces she'd sketched in the imaginary bus on the imaginary vacation.

"You can take your friends," she said softly.

Gwendolyn, who had been in the doorway for some time, cleared the lump from her throat.

"It's time to get dressed, Jenny. Come, children." Gwendolyn took their hands. "Let's go upstairs to Grandma Sarah."

"I'll be right up, Gwendolyn." Jenny went to the window. Half of Florence was gathered on the lawn. But the man she was searching for was still not there.

Claude Sullivan. Daniel's father.

Leaving the window, she went upstairs to don her wedding gown.

Music of harps filled his formal garden. A sea of gaily bedecked friends filled the chairs set up on the lawn. Flanked by Jenny's brothers, Daniel stood underneath the arch of yellow roses, waiting for his bride.

Victoria came first, her dark regal beauty causing a stir among the guests. More than one eligible bachelor was smitten that day by the maid of honor.

Patrick was next, bearing the ring carefully upon a satin pillow. Then Megan, spreading rose petals. Her next-door neighbor Bobby Newton, terror of the third grade, stuck out his tongue at her, and she stopped long enough to shake her fist in his face.

Then, acting as if the flower girl threatened guests every day, Megan smiled at her daddy and proceeded serenely down the aisle.

A glimpse of white satin caught Daniel's eye. Jenny. His love, his special angel. The sun shed its light across her face, but she didn't need the sun to shine. Jenny glowed with the beauty of spirit that made her glorious above all women.

Jenny smiled as only she could, and Daniel felt as breathless as he had the day he'd first seen her swinging in her flower garden with her white dress flying about her legs and her golden hair hiding her face. Breathless and reborn.

She came slowly, gliding along, with the gown hiding her limp.

"Do you take this woman to be your lawfully wedded wife?"

"I do." For all eternity. Loving his Jenny.

Jake Townsend kissed his daughter on the cheek and placed her hand in Daniel's. "Cherish her," he said.

"With all my heart."

There was a stir at the far end of the garden.

"Look, it's him," someone whispered.

Out of the corner of her eye Jenny saw Claude Sullivan. Without looking right or left, Claude strode through the crowd, straight down the center aisle. Daniel's hand tightened on hers.

"If anyone can show cause why this man should not be wed to this woman, let him speak now or forever hold his peace," the minister said.

There was a collective intake of breath as Claude took his place beside Daniel and glared at the minister. The harpist got nervous and plucked a harp string. A single clear note echoed in the stillness.

Father and son stared at each other, then slowly Claude held out his hand.

"If you'll still have me, I want to be a part of this family, Daniel."

Daniel took the outstretched hand. "I'll have you, Father. Gladly."

Jenny would never forget his smile. It was the greatest wedding gift she could ever receive.

"Well . . ." Claude turned to glare at the minister. "Are you going to stand there all day, or are you going to marry my son to this wonderful woman?"

"I'm going to marry them."

"Good. Get on with it."

"That's what I say. I'm tired of holding on to this basket." Megan grinned at her grandfather, a chip off the old block.

Daniel winked at Jenny. "This is a fiesty Irish family. Do you want to back out?"

"Never." Jenny smiled at him, then turned to smile sweetly at the minister. "Get on with it, please."

He did.

And with both their families and most of Florence looking on, Jenny Love-Townsend wed the man who had dared to become her hero.

FIFTEEN

Daniel knew the meaning of heaven, for every night he held it in his arms.

After a honeymoon in Paris, he and Jenny had settled into comfortable married bliss in his house in Florence. Gwendolyn was invited to join the household, but she declined, choosing instead to stay in the Victorian house that Jenny occasionally used as her studio.

Kicked back at his desk at Sullivan Enterprises, he counted himself the luckiest man alive. He had an adoring wife, two plucky children, a civil if not downright friendly relationship with Claire, and a business that wouldn't quit.

What more could a man want?

Helen punched the intercom. "Daniel, Clark Abrams on line two and your wife on line one."

Although he'd been waiting to hear from

Clark Abrams for three days, he punched line one first.

"Jenny? Hello, darling."

"Daniel..." Her breathy, lilting voice never ceased to send shivers of pleasure down his spine.

"I'm taking the children on a picnic this afternoon. Can you join us?"

"I'm sorry, sweetheart. I'll be tied up with Clark Abrams."

"The man who wants to buy you out."

Daniel laughed. "The man I'm going to buy out, darling."

"Good luck, Daniel."

She meant it too. Jenny never resented his work as Claire had.

A vision of her frolicking in the leaves with his children came to Daniel. He could almost feel the autumn sunshine on his face.

Would they miss him?

Daniel pushed the thought aside and punched line two. Clark Abrams was waiting.

He was late getting home, too late to sing a lullaby to his children, kiss their soft cheeks, and tuck them in. They had a mother to do all that now.

Jenny. She was sprawled in delicious disarray upon their bed, her golden hair shining in the lamplight, one of the sheer white gowns she favored tumbled off her shoulder to reveal one rose-tipped breast.

She came awake at his footsteps on the floor.

"Daniel?" Sleep made her voice throaty. And exceedingly sexy. Fully clothed, Daniel gathered his wife in his arms and buried his face in her sweet-smelling neck. "I didn't mean to fall asleep."

"I love waking you."

"And I love you waking me." She pressed against him, her body already quickened with need. "Wake me some more, Daniel."

Her artless sensuality inflamed his senses. He wanted to be inside her. Now.

Dangerous to lose all reason. Children were out of the question.

Jenny reached for his buttons, her hands hot upon his skin, robbing him of sanity. He crushed his mouth against hers, and they rolled together on the bed. He pushed aside her gown, found her hot, satiny sex. His fingers took up a wild rhythm.

"Oh, Daniel. I want to feel you, all of you. Now." Her hands were upon his zipper.

Need ripped at him, and urgency such as he'd never known.

"Wait, love . . ."

"Please, Daniel." She whimpered with the need that scorched through her.

Letting her go even for an instant was sheer agony. He fumbled in the bedside table, then seconds later, fully sheathed and fully clothed, he took them on a wild, hot journey that left them both panting.

Later, when he had undressed and lay beside her naked, he made love to her again, this time in the leisurely fashion of a man who knows he has the rest of his life with one special woman.

Negotiations with Clark Abrams demanded all his time and energy. As his body and his mind became more fatigued, his passion became more demanding. He spent the cool nights of October in hot, unbridled lovemaking.

Not only did Jenny anticipate his moods, she matched him. Once when she spread yellow rose petals and waited among them, naked, he was in her before he thought.

Her hot flesh squeezed at him, and he pulsed with life. He was lost, lost, riding the searing waves of passion.

"Daniel . . ." She called his name in the shattered voice that signaled she was nearing that final crashing climax.

The sound of his name electrified him. He levered himself quickly off.

"Daniel?"

"I wasn't ready, Jenny."

"Oh." Her voice was crushed with disappointment and defeat.

Daniel sat on the edge of the bed, silently damning the fates. Jenny put her small hand on his rigid back and rubbed away the tension.

"It's all right, Daniel," she whispered.

He took her in his arms, and sometime later, properly prepared and sensible, he made love to his wife.

Jenny slept with one hand curved under her cheek. The rosy flush of their recent coupling tinted her skin.

Daniel sat on the edge of the bed, studying her. His Jenny. His angel. How she loved him. How she trusted him.

He'd vowed never to fail her. But he almost had. Tonight.

Restless, he left their bedroom and wandered through the house. The children were sleeping peacefully; the animals were content. Every living thing in the house was content except Daniel.

Why? He had everything a man could want.

Sitting at his desk in the study, he idly riffled

through a coloring book one of the children had left behind. Out of its pages fell a drawing. One of Jenny's.

With only the light of the moon to see by, he studied the picture. In one corner of the page was their family, with all the names written underneath in Megan's uncertain cursive.

It was the opposite corner of the drawing that arrested Daniel's attention. He snapped on the light so he could see better.

Jenny had drawn a bus, and from all its windows hung animals and children—six children, not two. Megan and Patrick were easy to pick out, for even in caricature Jenny was precise. The other four were nameless, but they weren't unidentifiable. Each of them had the downy hair, the trusting smiles, and the slightly almond-shaped eyes of Down's syndrome. God's special children, riding in Jenny's dream bus. And underneath was the caption in large letters. *The Sullivan Family*.

The picture haunted Daniel for weeks. At odd moments—when he was talking with Clark Abrams or dictating to Helen or studying a balance sheet—he'd see Jenny's dream, fully illustrated on a drawing in a child's coloring book.

The figures on the profit and loss statement

stared back at him. He was a millionaire many times over. And a merger with Abrams would triple his wealth.

Jenny and the children were bird-watching today. Hoping to spot an eagle, Megan had said. And Jenny, knowing the importance of dreams, hadn't told her eagles were scarce in number, and not likely to be seen in Florence, Alabama, in any case.

"Let's take the binoculars so we can get a good look," Jenny had said instead.

He walked to the window, suddenly burning with the desire to see an eagle. He didn't see one, of course. All he saw was the vast parking lot and massive loading docks of Sullivan Enterprises. Signs of his success.

What more did he hope to prove?

Had Jenny and the children seen an eagle yet? He knew there had been a sighting once along the river.

"Daniel." Helen stuck her head around the door. "Mr. Abrams on line one."

Daniel reached for the phone, then changed his mind.

"Tell him I'm out," he said. When Helen shut the door, he picked up the phone and dialed Jenny's doctor.

"It's a simple procedure, Daniel." Dr. Wayne Dodge took off his glasses. "And irreversible. Are you sure about this?"

Daniel smiled. "I've never been more certain."

Dr. Dodge polished his glasses. "Have you talked to Jenny? Perhaps she should be the one to have it done."

"No! My decision is final."

"It's also noble, but then I've always known that about you, Daniel. You're a noble man. And Jenny is a very lucky woman."

Jenny and the children were flushed with the success of their bird-watching trip. They hadn't seen an eagle, but they'd spotted two red-winged blackbirds and a covey of quail.

Driving with great care as she always did, Jenny turned her car toward home.

"Look!" Patrick shouted, pointing.

Parked in front of the Sullivan mansion was the largest recreational vehicle Jenny had ever seen. It was white as a swan, with beautiful blue stripes running down the sides and blue-and-white-checked curtains in the windows.

"It's a bus." Megan jumped up and down in her excitement. "Who is it, Jenny? Uncle William?"

William was the one of her brothers who would do something like that, go off and buy a bus.

"I don't know." Such a beautiful bus. Jenny hoped it did belong to William. Then she'd get to ride.

The children barreled out of the car the minute Jenny parked. And around the corner of the bus came Daniel.

"Daddy! Daddy!" they yelled, catapulting into his arms. "Whose bus?"

Hugging them close, he gazed over the top of their heads at Jenny.

"Jenny's," he said.

Jenny wondered if it was possible to die of joy. She thought she might. With her hands pressed over her heart she gazed at her husband, too overcome to speak.

"Can we ride?" Megan asked.

"You certainly can."

"Where will we go?" Megan, ever practical, wanted answers.

"Wherever Jenny wants to."

The children raced off to inspect the bus. Jenny came to him then, hurrying as fast as her brave rolling gait would allow, hurrying straight into his arms. He kissed her upturned face.

"You remembered," she whispered.

"It's high time." He kissed her eyelids, her hair, her ears, her cheek, her chin. "We'll see the world, Jenny. We'll stop at every mountain and every stream in America."

"What about your work?"

"I'm selling out."

"Selling? Daniel . . . not for me."

"Partly for you, partly for me, but mostly for the children." The children of her heart. Megan and Patrick. Only two in such a big bus when there was so much room for more.

Oh, there she was again. Dreaming impossible dreams. Daniel and Megan and Patrick were all she needed.

"I think six children will need a full-time father, don't you, Jenny?" Daniel tipped her face up, smiling at her.

"Six? But, Daniel . . ."

"Shh." He kissed her once more. "Nothing is impossible, Jenny."

Sitting side by side in the adoption agency, Daniel and Jenny held hands and listened to the bad news.

"There is a waiting list of about two years." Mrs. Lorene Henley restacked a set of file folders threatening to topple off the edge of her desk. Her frizzy hair stuck out around her head like a scrub pad and her brow was drawn together in a perpetual frown. She was overworked and understaffed.

"So long?" Jenny said.

"I'm sorry. You'd be amazed at the childless couples standing in line for a strong, healthy baby." She liked Daniel and Jenny Sullivan. Not only liked them, but wanted to help them. If only there were a way.

"Do you have others?" Daniel's voice was quiet, determined.

And suddenly Lorene Henley knew the way.

"There is one child ... three years old." She scrambled through the stack of folders, pulled out a photograph, and handed it to Daniel and Jenny.

A little boy with a cherub's face and big dark eyes smiled back at them. He had the dusky skin of his Spanish mother, the curly hair of his Scottish father, and a determined little chin all his own. He was seated in a rocking horse with one leg firmly in the stirrup—and one leg missing.

"His name is Kevin," Lorene said. "Nobody wants him."

Jenny and Daniel gazed at the small homeless child and then at each other.

"We do," they said.

EPILOGUE

Megan had nicknamed the bus Rover.

Rover was well traveled and dusty, his springs sagging and his upholstery wanting a good cleaning from all the peanut butter and jelly stains. In spite of his shortcomings, Rover was staunch.

He rocked down the road, carrying his lively crew. Kevin, six years old and growing like a weed, had the voice of an angel. He was leading his brothers and sisters in a tune he'd learned at kindergarten. Clayton and Randy couldn't say the words right and might never be able to, but that didn't stop them from trying. They sang with all the fervor of four-year-olds who knew that extravagant praise would be forthcoming from their parents.

Baby Sally would never hear the music, but

she smiled up at her mother anyway. She understood love.

Megan and Patrick, who prided themselves on being the oldest, tried not to drown out the little ones with their singing. Irish to the tips of their toes, they had their father's good voice and his fondness for song.

"Join in, Daddy!" Kevin yelled.

The other children took up the cry. "Yeah, Daddy! Join in!"

Daniel pulled the bus to a stop in a small forest glade and joined his children's song. The lines of worry that had once creased his face had disappeared. He laughed and sang a lot now. And loved.

A flush crept into Jenny's face. Oh, how he loved.

Cuddling her baby close, she listened to the voice of her husband singing to his happy children.

It took a special man to share love with children nobody else wanted. But then what had she expected of a man who loved a woman nobody else dared love?

Daniel glanced at her, his eyes twinkling, and she gave him a small secret smile.

THE EDITOR'S CORNER

There's never too much of a good thing when it comes to romances inspired by beloved stories, so next month we present TREASURED TALES II. Coming your way are six brand-new LOVESWEPTs written by some of the most talented authors of romantic fiction today. You'll delight in their contemporary versions of age-old classics... and experience the excitement and passion of falling in love. TREASURED TALES II—what a way to begin the new year!

The first book in our fabulous line up is **PERFECT DOUBLE** by Cindy Gerard, LOVESWEPT #660. In this wonderful retelling of *The Prince and the Pauper* business mogul Logan Prince gets saved by a stranger from a near-fatal mugging, then wakes up in an unfamiliar bed to find a reluctant angel with a siren's body bandaging his wounds! Logan vows to win Carmen Sanchez's heart—

even if it means making a daring bargain with his look-alike rescuer and trading places with the cowboy drifter. It take plenty of wooing before Carmen surrenders to desire—and even more sweet persuasion to regain her trust once he confesses to his charade. A top-notch story from talented Cindy.

Homer's epic poem *The Odyssey* has never been as romantic as Billie Green's version, **BABY, COME BACK**, LOVESWEPT #661. Like Odysseus, David Moore has spent a long time away from home. Finally free after six years in captivity, and with an unrecognizable face and voice, he's not sure if there's still room for him in the lives of his sweet wife, Kathy, and their son, Ben. When he returns home, he masquerades as a handyman, determined to be close to his son, aching to show his wife that, though she's now a successful businesswoman, she still needs him. Poignant and passionate, this love story shows Billie at her finest!

Tom Falconson lives the nightmare of *The Invisible Man* in Terry Lawrence's **THE SHADOW LOVER**, LOVESWEPT #662. When a government experiment goes awry and renders the dashingly virile intelligence agent invisible, Tom knows he has only one person to turn to. Delighted by mysteries, ever in search of the unexplained, Alice Willow opens her door to him, offering him refuge and the sensual freedom to pull her dangerously close. But even as Tom sets out to show her that the phantom in her arms is a flesh-and-blood man, he wonders if their love is strong enough to prove that nothing is impossible. Terry provides plenty of thrills and tempestuous emotions in this fabulous tale.

In Jan Hudson's **FLY WITH ME**, LOVESWEPT #663, Sawyer Hayes is a modern-day Peter Pan who soars through the air in a gleaming helicopter. He touches down in Pip LeBaron's backyard with an offer of a job in his company, but the computer genius quickly informs him that for now she's doing nothing except making up for the childhood she missed. Bewitched by her delicate beauty, Sawyer decides to help her, though her kissable mouth persuades him that a few grown-up games would be more fun. Pip soon welcomes his tantalizing embrace, turning to liquid moonlight beneath his touch. But is there a future together for a man who seems to live for fun and a lady whose work has been her whole life? Jan weaves her magic in this enchanting romance.

"The Ugly Duckling" was Linda Cajio's inspiration for her new LOVESWEPT, **HE'S SO SHY,** #664—and if there ever was an ugly duckling, Richard Creighton was it. Once a skinny nerd with glasses, he's now impossibly sexy, irresistibly gorgeous, and the hottest actor on the big screen. Penelope Marsh can't believe that this leading man in her cousin's movie is the same person she went to grade school with. She thinks he's definitely out of her league, but Richard doesn't agree. Drawn to the willowy schoolteacher, Richard dares her to accept what's written in the stars—that she's destined to be his leading lady for life. Linda delivers a surefire hit.

Last, but certainly not least, is **ANIMAL MAGNETISM** by Bonnie Pega, LOVESWEPT #665. Only Dr. Dolittle is Sebastian Kent's equal when it comes to relating to animals—but Danni Sullivan insists the veterinarian still needs her help. After all, he's new in her hometown, and no one knows every cat, bull, and pig there as well as she. For once giving in to impulse, Sebastian hires her on the spot—then thinks twice about it when her touch arouses long-denied yearnings. He can charm any beast, but he definitely needs a lesson in how to soothe his wounded heart. And Danni has just the right touch to heal his pain—and make him believe in love once more. Bonnie will delight you with this thoroughly enchanting story.

Happy reading!

With warmest wishes,

Nita Taublib

Nita Taublib

Associate Publisher

P.S. Don't miss the fabulous women's fiction Bantam has coming in January: **DESIRE**, the newest novel from bestselling author Amanda Quick; **LONG TIME COMING,** Sandra Brown's classic contemporary romance; **STRANGER IN MY ARMS** by R. J. Kaiser, a novel of romantic suspense in which a woman who has lost her memory is in danger of also losing her life; and **WHERE DOLPHINS GO** by LOVESWEPT author Peggy Webb, a truly unique romance that integrates into its story the fascinating ability of dolphins to aid injured children. We'll be giving you a sneak peek at these wonderful books in next month's LOVESWEPTs. And immediately following this page, look for a preview of the exciting women's novels from Bantam that are *available now!*

Don't miss these exciting books by your favorite Bantam authors

On sale in November:

ADAM'S FALL
by Sandra Brown

NOTORIOUS
by Patricia Potter

PRINCESS OF THIEVES
by Katherine O'Neal

CAPTURE THE NIGHT
by Geralyn Dawson

And in hardcover from Doubleday
ON WINGS OF MAGIC
by Kay Hooper

Adam's Fall

Available this month in hardcover
from *New York Times*
bestselling author

SANDRA BROWN

Over the past few years, Lilah Mason had watched her sister Elizabeth find love, get married, and have children, while she's been more than content to channel her energies into a career. A physical therapist with an unsinkable spirit and unwavering compassion, she's one of the best in the field. But when Lilah takes on a demanding new case, her patient's life isn't the only one transformed. She's never had a tougher patient than Adam, who challenges her methods and authority at every turn. Yet Lilah is determined to help him recover the life he's lost. What she can't see is that while she's winning Adam's battle, she's losing her heart. Now, as professional duty and passionate yearnings clash, Lilah must choose the right course for them both.

Sizzling Romance from One of the World's Hottest Pens

Winner of *Romantic Times*'s
1992 Storyteller of the Year Award

Patricia Potter

Nationally bestselling author of
Renegade and **Lightning**

NOTORIOUS

The owner of the most popular saloon in San Francisco, Catalina Hilliard knows Marsh Canton is trouble the moment she first sees him. He's not the first to attempt to open a rival saloon next door to the Silver Slipper, but he does possess a steely strength that was missing from the men she'd driven out of business. Even more perilous to Cat's plans is the spark of desire that flares between them, a desire that's about to spin her carefully orchestrated life out of control . . .

"We have nothing to discuss," she said coldly, even as she struggled to keep from trembling. All her thoughts were in disarray. He was so adept at personal invasion. That look in his eyes of pure radiance, of physical need, almost burned through her.

Fifteen years. Nearly fifteen years since a man had touched her so intimately. And he was doing it only with his eyes!

And, dear Lucifer, she was responding.

She'd thought herself immune from desire. If she'd ever had any, she believed it had been killed long ago by brutality and shame and utter abhorrence of an act that gave men power and left her little more than a thing to be used and hurt. She'd never felt this bubbling, boiling warmth inside, this craving that was more than physical hunger.

That's what frightened her most of all.

But she wouldn't show it. She would never show it! She didn't even like Canton, devil take him. She didn't like anything about him. And she would send him back to wherever he came. Tail between his legs. No matter what it took. And she would never feel desire again.

But now she had little choice, unless she wished to stand here all afternoon, his hand burning a brand into her. He wasn't going to let her go, and perhaps it was time to lay her cards on the table. She preferred open warfare to guerrilla fighting. She hadn't felt right about the kidnapping and beating—even if she did frequently regret her moment of mercy on his behalf.

She shrugged and his hand relaxed slightly. They left, and he flagged down a carriage for hire. Using those strangely elegant manners that still puzzled her, he helped her inside with a grace that would put royalty to shame.

He left her then for a moment and spoke to the driver, passing a few bills up to him, then returned and vaulted to the seat next to her. Hard-muscled thigh pushed against her leg; his tanned arm, made visible by the rolled-up sleeve, touched her much smaller one, the wiry male hair brushing against her skin, sparking a thousand tiny charges. His scent, a spicy mixture of bay and soap, teased her senses. Everything about him—the strength and power and raw masculinity that he made no attempt to conceal—made her feel fragile, delicate.

But not vulnerable, she told herself. Never vulnerable again. She would fight back by seizing control and keeping it.

She straightened her back and smiled. A seductive smile. A smile that had entranced men for the last ten years. A practiced smile that knew exactly how far to go. A kind of promise that left doors opened, while permitting retreat. It was a smile that kept men coming to the Silver Slipper even as they understood they had no real chance of realizing the dream.

Canton raised an eyebrow. "You *are* very good," he said admiringly.

She shrugged. "It usually works."

"I imagine it does," he said. "Although I doubt if most of the men you use it on have seen the thornier part of you."

"Most don't irritate me as you do."

"Irritate, Miss Cat?"

"Don't call me Cat. My name is Catalina."

"Is it?"

"Is yours really Taylor Canton?"

The last two questions were spoken softly, dangerously, both trying to probe weaknesses, and both recognizing the tactic of the other.

"I would swear to it on a Bible," Marsh said, his mouth quirking.

"I'm surprised you have one, or know what one is."

"I had a very good upbringing, Miss Cat." He emphasized the last word.

"And then what happened?" she asked caustically.

The sardonic amusement in his eyes faded. "A great deal. And what is your story?"

Dear God, his voice was mesmerizing, an intimate song that said nothing but wanted everything. Low and deep and provocative. Compelling. And irresistible . . . almost.

"I had a very poor upbringing," she said. "And then a great deal happened."

For the first time since she'd met him, she saw real humor in his eyes. Not just that cynical amusement as if he were some higher being looking down on a world inhabited by silly children. "You're the first woman I've met with fewer scruples than my own," he said, admiration again in his voice.

She opened her eyes wide. "You have some?"

"As I told you that first night, I don't usually mistreat women."

"Usually?"

"Unless provoked."

"A threat, Mr. Canton?"

"I never threaten, Miss Cat. Neither do I turn down challenges."

"And you usually win?"

"Not usually, Miss Cat. Always." The word was flat. Almost ugly in its surety.

"So do I," she said complacently.

Their voices, Cat knew, had lowered into little more than husky whispers. The air in the closed carriage was sparking, hissing, crackling. Threatening to ignite. His hand moved to her arm, his fingers running up and down it in slow, caressingly sensuous trails.

And then the heat surrounding them was as intense as that in the heart of a volcano. Intense and violent. She wondered very briefly if this was a version of hell. She had just decided it was when he bent toward her, his lips brushing over hers.

And heaven and hell collided.

PRINCESS OF THIEVES
by
Katherine O'Neal

"A brilliant new talent bound to make her mark on the genre."
—Iris Johansen

Mace Blackwood is the greatest con artist in the world, a demon whose family is responsible for the death of Saranda Sherwin's parents. And though he might be luring her to damnation itself, Saranda allows herself to be set aflame by the fire in his dark eyes. It's a calculated surrender that he finds both intoxicating and infuriating, for one evening alone with the blue-eyed siren can never be enough. And now he will stop at nothing to have her forever....

Saranda could read his intentions in the gleam of his midnight eyes. "Stay away from me," she gasped.

"Surely, you're not afraid of me? I've already admitted defeat."

"As if I'd trust anything you'd say."

Mace raised a brow. "Trust? No, sweetheart, it's not about trust between us."

"You're right. It's about a battle between our families that has finally come to an end. The

Sherwins have won, Blackwood. You have no further hand to play."

Even as she said it, she knew it wasn't true. Despite the bad blood between them, they had unfinished business. Because the game, this time, had gone too far.

"That's separate. The feud, the competition—that has nothing to do with what's happening between you and me."

"You must think I'm the rankest kind of amateur. Do you think I don't know what you're up to?"

He put his hand to her cheek and stroked the softly shadowed contours of her face. "What am I up to?"

He was so close, she could feel the muscles of his chest toying with her breasts. Against all sense, she hungered to be touched.

"If you can succeed in seducing me, you can run to Winston with the news—"

His hand drifted from her cheek down the naked column of her neck, to softly caress the slope of her naked shoulder. "I could tell him you slept with me whether you do or not. But you know as well as I do he wouldn't believe me."

"That argument won't work either, Blackwood," she said in a dangerously breathy tone.

"Very well, Miss Sherwin. Why don't we just lay our cards on the table?"

"Why not indeed?"

"Then here it is. I don't like you any more than you like me. In fact, I can't think of a woman I'd be less likely to covet. My family cared for yours no more than yours cared for mine. But I find myself in the unfortunate circumstance of wanting you to distraction. For some reason I can't even fathom, I can't look at you without wondering what you'd look like panting in my arms. Without wanting to feel your naked skin beneath my hands. Or taste your sweat on my tongue. Without needing to come inside you and make you cry out in passion and lose some of that *goddamned* control." A faint moan escaped her throat. "You're all I think about. You're like a fever in my brain. I keep thinking if I took you *just once*, I might finally expel you from my mind. So I don't suppose either of us is leaving this office before we've had what you came for."

"I came to tell you—"

"You could have done that any time. You could have left me wondering for the rest of the night if the wedding would take place. But you didn't wait. You knew if this was going to happen, it had to be tonight. Because once you're Winston's wife, I won't come near you. The minute you say 'I do,' you and I take off the gloves, darling, and the real battle begins. So it's now or never." He lowered his mouth to her shoulder, and her breath left her in a sigh.

"Now or never," she repeated in a daze.

"One night to forget who we are and what it all means. You're so confident of winning. Surely, you wouldn't deny me the spoils of the game. Or more to the point . . . deny yourself."

She looked up and met his sweltering gaze. After three days of not seeing him, she'd forgotten how devastatingly handsome he was. "I shan't fall in love with you, if that's what you're thinking. This will give you no advantage over me. I'm still going after you with both barrels loaded."

"Stop trying so hard to figure it out. I don't give a hang what you think of me. And I don't need your tender mercy. I tell you point-blank, if you think you've won, you may be in for a surprise. But that's beside the point." He wrapped a curl around his finger. Then, taking the pins from her hair, one by one, he dropped them to the floor. She felt her taut nerves jump as each pin clicked against the tile.

He ran both hands through the silvery hair, fluffing it with his fingers, dragging them slowly through the length as he watched the play of light on the silky strands. It spilled like moonlight over her shoulders. "Did you have to be so beautiful?" he rasped.

"Do you have to look so much like a Blackwood?"

He looked at her for a moment, his eyes piercing hers, his hands tangled in her hair. "Tell me what you want."

She couldn't look at him. It brought back memories of his brother she'd rather not relive. As it was, she couldn't believe she was doing this. But she had to have him. It was as elemental as food for her body and air to breathe. Her eyes dropped to his mouth—that blatant, sexual mouth that could make her wild with a grin or wet with a word.

She closed her eyes. If she didn't look at him, maybe she could separate this moment from the past. From what his brother had done. Her voice was a mere whisper when she spoke. "I want you to stop wasting time," she told him, "and make love to me."

He let go of her hair and took her naked shoulders in his hands. Bending her backward, he brought his mouth to hers with a kiss so searing, it scalded her heart.

CAPTURE THE NIGHT

by Geralyn Dawson

Award-winning author of

The Texan's Bride

"My highest praise goes to this author and her work, one of the best... I have read in years."
—*Rendezvous*

A desperate French beauty, the ruggedly handsome Texan who rescues her, and their precious stolen "Rose" are swept together by destiny as they each try to escape the secrets of their past.

Madeline groaned as the man called Sinclair sauntered toward her. This is all I need, she thought.

He stopped beside her and dipped into a perfect imitation of a gentleman's bow. Eyes shining, he looked up and said in his deplorable French, "Madame, do you by chance speak English? Apparently, we'll be sharing a spot in line. I beg to make your acquaintance."

She didn't answer.

He sighed and straightened. Then a wicked grin creased his face and in English he drawled, "Brazos Sinclair's my name, Texas born and bred. Most of my friends call me Sin, especially my lady friends. Nobody calls me Claire but once. I'll be sailin' with you on the *Uriel*."

Madeline ignored him.

Evidently, that bothered him not at all. "Cute baby," he said, peeking past the blanket. "Best keep him covered good though. This weather'll chill him."

Madeline bristled at the implied criticism. She glared at the man named Sin.

His grin faded. "Sure you don't speak English?"

She held her silence.

"Guess not, huh. That's all right, I'll enjoy conversin' with you anyway." He shot a piercing glare toward Victor Considérant, the colonists' leader and the man who had refused him a place on the *Uriel*. "I need a diversion, you see. Otherwise I'm liable to do something I shouldn't." Angling his head, he gave her another sweeping gaze. "You're a right fine lookin' woman, ma'am, a real beauty. Don't know that I think much of your husband, though, leavin' you here on the docks by your lonesome."

He paused and looked around, his stare snagging on a pair of scruffy sailors. "It's a dangerous thing for women to be alone in such a place, and for a beautiful one like you, well, I hesitate to think."

Obviously, Madeline said to herself.

The Texan continued, glancing around at the people milling along the wharf. " 'Course, I can't say I understand you Europeans. I've been here goin' on two years, and I'm no closer to figurin' y'all out now than I was the day I rolled off the boat." He reached into his jacket pocket and pulled out a pair of peppermint sticks.

Madeline declined the offer by shaking her head, and he returned one to his pocket before taking a slow lick of the second. "One thing, there's all those kings and royals. I think it's nothin' short of silly to climb on a high horse simply because blood family's been plowin' the same dirt for hundreds of years. I tell you what, ma'am, Texans aren't built for bowin'. It's been bred right out of us."

Brazos leveled a hard stare on Victor Considérant and shook his peppermint in the Frenchman's direction. "And aristocrats are just as bad as royalty. That fellow's one of the worst. Although I'll admit that his head's on right about kings and all, his whole notion to create a socialistic city in the heart of Texas is just plain stupid."

Gesturing toward the others who waited ahead of them in line, he said, "Look around you, lady. I'd lay odds not more than a dozen of these folks know the first little bit about farmin', much less what it takes for survivin' on the frontier. Take that crate, for instance." He shook his head incredulously, "They've stored work tools with violins for an ocean crossing, for goodness sake. These folks don't have the sense to pour rain water from a boot!" He popped the candy into his mouth, folded his arms across his chest, and studied the ship, chewing in a pensive silence.

The nerve of the man, Madeline thought, gritting her teeth against the words she'd love to speak. Really, to comment on another's intelligence when his own is so obviously lacking. Listen to his French.

And his powers of observation. Why, she knew how she looked.

Beautiful wasn't the appropriate word.

Brazos swallowed his candy and said, "Hmm. You've given me an idea." Before Madeline gathered her wits to stop him, he leaned over and kissed her cheek. "Thanks, Beauty. And listen, you take care out here without a man to protect you. If I see your husband on this boat I'm goin' to give him a piece of my mind about leavin' you alone." He winked and left her, walking toward the gangway.

Madeline touched the sticky spot on her cheek damp from his peppermint kiss and watched, fascinated despite herself, as the over-bold Texan tapped Considérant on the shoulder. In French that grated on her ears, he said. "Listen Frenchman, I'll make a deal with you. If you find a place for me on your ship I'll be happy to share my extensive knowledge of Texas with any of your folks who'd be interested in learnin'. This land you bought on the Trinity River—it's not more than half a day's ride from my cousin's spread. I've spent a good deal of time in that area over the past few years. I can tell you all about it."

"Mr. Sinclair," Considérant said in English, "please do not further abuse my language. I chose that land myself. Personally. I can answer any questions my peers may have about our new home. Now, as I have told you, this packet has been chartered to sail La Réunion colonists exclusively. Every space is assigned. I sympathize with your need to return to your home, but unfortunately the *Uriel* cannot accommodate you. Please excuse me, Monsieur Sinclair. I have much to see to before we sail. Good day."

"Good day my—" Brazos bit off his words. He turned abruptly and stomped away from the ship. Halting before Madeline, he declared, "This boat ain't leavin' until morning. It's not over yet. By General Taylor's tailor, when it sails, I'm gonna be on it."

He flashed a victorious grin and drawled, "Honey, you've captured my heart and about three other parts. I'll look forward to seein' you aboard ship."

As he walked away, she dropped a handsome gold pocket watch into her reticule, then called out to him in crisp, King's English. "Better you had offered your brain for ballast, Mr. Sinclair. Perhaps then you'd have been allowed aboard the *Uriel*."

And don't miss these spectacular
romances from Bantam Books,
on sale in December

DESIRE
by the nationally bestselling author
Amanda Quick

LONG TIME COMING
a classic romance by the
New York Times
bestselling author
Sandra Brown

STRANGER IN MY ARMS
a thrilling novel of romantic suspense
by **R. J. Kaiser**

WHERE DOLPHINS GO
by bestselling LOVESWEPT author
Peggy Webb
"Ms. Webb has an inventive mind brimming
with originality that makes all of her
books special reading."
—*Romantic Times*

And in hardcover from Doubleday

AMAZON LILY
by *Theresa Weir*
"Romantic adventure has no finer writer than
the spectacular Theresa Weir."
—*Romantic Times*

CALL JAN SPILLER'S ASTROLINE

DAILY PERSONALIZED PREDICTIONS!

ONLY FORECAST OF ITS KIND!

This is totally different from any horoscope you've ever heard and is the most authentic astrology forecast available by phone! Gain insight into LOVE, MONEY, HEALTH, WORK.

Empower yourself with this amazing astrology forecast. Let our intuitive tarot readings reveal with uncanny insight your personal destiny and the destinies of those close to you.

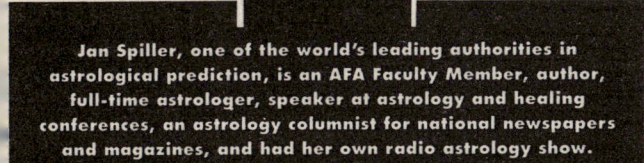

Jan Spiller, one of the world's leading authorities in astrological prediction, is an AFA Faculty Member, author, full-time astrologer, speaker at astrology and healing conferences, an astrology columnist for national newspapers and magazines, and had her own radio astrology show.

1-900-903-8000 ★ ASTROLOGY FORECAST
1-900-903-9000 ★ TAROT READING
99¢ For The First Min. ★ $1.75 For Each Add'l. Min. ★ Average Length Of Call 7 Min.

CALL NOW AND FIND OUT WHAT THE STARS HAVE IN STORE FOR YOU TODAY!
All 24 hours a day, 7 days a week. You must be 18 years or older to call and have a touch tone phone. Astral Marketing 1-702-251-1415.

DHS 7/93

OFFICIAL RULES

To enter the sweepstakes below carefully follow all instructions found elsewhere in this offer.

The **Winners Classic** will award prizes with the following approximate maximum values: 1 Grand Prize: $26,500 (or $25,000 cash alternate); 1 First Prize: $3,000; 5 Second Prizes: $400 each; 35 Third Prizes: $100 each; 1,000 Fourth Prizes: $7.50 each. Total maximum retail value of Winners Classic Sweepstakes is $42,500. Some presentations of this sweepstakes may contain individual entry numbers corresponding to one or more of the aforementioned prize levels. To determine the Winners, individual entry numbers will first be compared with the winning numbers preselected by computer. For winning numbers not returned, prizes will be awarded in random drawings from among all eligible entries received. Prize choices may be offered at various levels. If a winner chooses an automobile prize, all license and registration fees, taxes, destination charges and, other expenses not offered herein are the responsibility of the winner. If a winner chooses a trip, travel must be complete within one year from the time the prize is awarded. Minors must be accompanied by an adult. Travel companion(s) must also sign release of liability. Trips are subject to space and departure availability. Certain black-out dates may apply.

The following applies to the sweepstakes named above:

No purchase necessary. You can also enter the sweepstakes by sending your name and address to: P.O. Box 508, Gibbstown, N.J. 08027. Mail each entry separately. Sweepstakes begins 6/1/93. Entries must be received by 12/30/94. Not responsible for lost, late, damaged, misdirected, illegible or postage due mail. Mechanically reproduced entries are not eligible. All entries become property of the sponsor and will not be returned.

Prize Selection/Validations: Selection of winners will be conducted no later than 5:00 PM on January 28, 1995, by an independent judging organization whose decisions are final. Random drawings will be held at 1211 Avenue of the Americas, New York, N.Y. 10036. Entrants need not be present to win. Odds of winning are determined by total number of entries received. Circulation of this sweepstakes is estimated not to exceed 200 million. All prizes are guaranteed to be awarded and delivered to winners. Winners will be notified by mail and may be required to complete an affidavit of eligibility and release of liability which must be returned within 14 days of date on notification or alternate winners will be selected in a random drawing. Any prize notification letter or any prize returned to a participating sponsor, Bantam Doubleday Dell Publishing Group, Inc., its participating divisions or subsidiaries, or the independent judging organization as undeliverable will be awarded to an alternate winner. Prizes are not transferable. No substitution for prizes except as offered or as may be necessary due to unavailability, in which case a prize of equal or greater value will be awarded. Prizes will be awarded approximately 90 days after the drawing. All taxes are the sole responsibility of the winners. Entry constitutes permission (except where prohibited by law) to use winners' names, hometowns, and likenesses for publicity purposes without further or other compensation. Prizes won by minors will be awarded in the name of parent or legal guardian.

Participation: Sweepstakes open to residents of the United States and Canada, except for the province of Quebec. Sweepstakes sponsored by Bantam Doubleday Dell Publishing Group, Inc., (BDD), 1540 Broadway, New York, NY 10036. Versions of this sweepstakes with different graphics and prize choices will be offered in conjunction with various solicitations or promotions by different subsidiaries and divisions of BDD. Where applicable, winners will have their choice of any prize offered at level won. Employees of BDD, its divisions, subsidiaries, advertising agencies, independent judging organization, and their immediate family members are not eligible.

Canadian residents, in order to win, must first correctly answer a time limited arithmetical skill testing question. Void in Puerto Rico, Quebec and wherever prohibited or restricted by law. Subject to all federal, state, local and provincial laws and regulations. For a list of major prize winners (available after 1/29/95): send a self-addressed, stamped envelope entirely separate from your entry to: Sweepstakes Winners, P.O. Box 517, Gibbstown, NJ 08027. Requests must be received by 12/30/94. DO NOT SEND ANY OTHER CORRESPONDENCE TO THIS P.O. BOX.

SWP 7/93

Don't miss these fabulous Bantam women's fiction titles

now on sale

• NOTORIOUS
by Patricia Potter, author of *RENEGADE*
Long ago, Catalina Hilliard had vowed never to give away her heart, but she hadn't counted on the spark of desire that flared between her and her business rival, Marsh Canton. Now that desire is about to spin Cat's carefully orchestrated life out of control.

_____56225-8 $5.50/6.50 in Canada

• PRINCESS OF THIEVES
by Katherine O'Neal, author of *THE LAST HIGHWAYMAN*
Mace Blackwood was a daring rogue—the greatest con artist in the world. Saranda Sherwin was a master thief who used her wits and wiles to make tough men weak. And when Saranda's latest charade leads to tragedy and sends her fleeing for her life, Mace is compelled to follow, no matter what the cost.

_____56066-2 $5.50/$6.50 in Canada

• CAPTURE THE NIGHT
by Geralyn Dawson
In this "Once Upon a Time" Romance with "Beauty and the Beast" at its heart, Geralyn Dawson weaves the love story of a runaway beauty, the Texan who rescues her, and their precious stolen "Rose."

_____56176-6 $4.99/5.99 in Canada

Ask for these books at your local bookstore or use this page to order.

❑ Please send me the books I have checked above. I am enclosing $ _____ (add $2.50 to cover postage and handling). Send check or money order, no cash or C. O. D.'s please.

Name _____

Address _____

City/ State/ Zip _____

Send order to: Bantam Books, Dept. FN123, 2451 S. Wolf Rd., Des Plaines, IL 60018
Allow four to six weeks for delivery.
Prices and availability subject to change without notice.

Don't miss these fabulous Bantam women's fiction titles

on sale in December

- **DESIRE** by Amanda Quick, *New York Times* bestselling author of DECEPTION

  "Quick has provided an inviting little world...A featherlight, warmhearted fantasy...Fans will welcome this perfect little popover of a romance."—Kirkus Reviews ___56153-7 *$5.99/$6.99 in Canada*

- **LONG TIME COMING** by Sandra Brown, *New York Times* bestselling author of *Temperatures Rising* and *French Silk*

  "Ms. Brown's larger than life heroes and heroines make you believe in all the warm, wonderful, wild things in life."
  —Rendezvous ___56278-9 *$4.99/$5.99 in Canada*

- **ALL MY SINS REMEMBERED** by Rosie Thomas

  "A compelling and moving story...full of wisdom and caring."
  —The Washington Post Book World___56368-8 *$5.99/$6.99 n Canada*

- **STRANGER IN MY ARMS** by R. J. Kaiser

  With no recollection of who she was, Hillary Bass became spellbound by a love she couldn't resist...and haunted by a murder she couldn't recall... ___56251-7 *$4.99/$5.99 in Canada*

- **WHERE DOLPHINS GO** by Peggy Webb

  She was a mother looking for a miracle, he was a doctor looking to forget. The last thing they expected was to find each other.
  ___56056-5 *$5.99/$6.99 n Canada*

Ask for these books at your local bookstore or use this page to order.

☐ Please send me the books I have checked above. I am enclosing $ _____ (add $2.50 to cover postage and handling). Send check or money order, no cash or C. O. D.'s please.

Name _____

Address _____

City/ State/ Zip _____

Send order to: Bantam Books, Dept. FN124, 2451 S. Wolf Rd., Des Plaines, IL 60018

Allow four to six weeks for delivery.

Prices and availability subject to change without notice.

FN124 12/93